AFTER

AFTER

Anna Patrick

Copyright © 2024 Anna Patrick

The moral right of the author has been asserted.

Apart from any fair dealing for the purposes of research or private study, or criticism or review, as permitted under the Copyright, Designs and Patents Act 1988, this publication may only be reproduced, stored or transmitted, in any form or by any means, with the prior permission in writing of the publishers, or in the case of reprographic reproduction in accordance with the terms of licences issued by the Copyright Licensing Agency. Enquiries concerning reproduction outside those terms should be sent to the publishers.

This is a work of fiction. Names, characters, businesses, places, events and incidents are either the products of the author's imagination or used in a fictitious manner. Any resemblance to actual persons, living or dead, or actual events is purely coincidental.

Troubador Publishing Ltd
Unit E2 Airfield Business Park,
Harrison Road, Market Harborough,
Leicestershire LE16 7UL
Tel: 0116 279 2299
Email: books@troubador.co.uk
Web: www.troubador.co.uk

ISBN 978-1-80514-339-0

British Library Cataloguing in Publication Data.
A catalogue record for this book is available from the British Library.

Printed and bound in the UK by TJ Books Limited, Padstow, Cornwall
Typeset in 11pt Sabon LT Pro by Troubador Publishing Ltd, Leicester, UK

For Sorcha

PREFACE

WHEN A FRIEND READING the first draft of this book asked if my intention was to exonerate the Gestapo, I nearly scrapped the entire project. Absolutely not. The immense suffering caused by the Gestapo throughout occupied Europe cannot be excused or justified.

So why write a novel with an ex-Gestapo officer as its protagonist?

In 2019, I published *No Going Back*, which told my mother's story of arrest and interrogation by the Gestapo in Poland before being sent to Ravensbrück concentration camp.

Despite carrying a gun for the Resistance, my mother was never tortured. I knew her story, or most of it, but what lay behind her relatively benign interrogation? She was beaten but not systematically tortured. Did they believe her extraordinary cover story or was she just lucky? My mother credited divine intervention for her good fortune, but I needed a better plot device.

During my research, I discovered that many of the detectives from the German Criminal Police, the so-called Kripo or Kriminalpolizei, moved across to the Gestapo. Some of them, possibly very few, remained career detectives and did not resort to torture.

For example, the detectives who questioned Sophie Scholl of the White Rose resistance movement in Germany did so without physical violence. This did not prevent her execution by guillotine after a show trial, but she was not tortured beforehand.

Gradually, the figure of Inspector Heinz Bauer developed in my mind. He would be a career detective who joined the Gestapo but abhorred their methods and did not resort to torture. He was the man I put in charge of my mother's arrest and interrogation.

In the way fictional characters become real to you, I pondered his character and motivation. After the book was published, he lingered in my thoughts, and I continued to wonder about him and his family and what would have happened to them as the Second World War ended.

After is the result of those wonderings.

CHAPTER 1

SOMEONE WAS AFTER HIM. Clever. Relentless. Heinz Bauer had already doubled back, but the pursuer was on his heels. He cursed under his breath. Sweat streamed down his back. This wasn't his territory: he'd always been a city detective. He longed for streets; crowds; a reflection in a shop window; the chance to glance in a parked car's mirror; a passer-by forced into the road. He needed clues to mean something, instead of this endless shadowy forest where he was the prey.

A sharp crack to his right veered him to the left. He tripped over a moss-covered root and fell with a groan. It was over. Frustration jabbed him as painfully as the stitch in his side. What was it to be? A speedy death or a lengthy prison sentence? Forcing himself up, he turned expecting to see a gun in his face.

'Heil Hitler'

Bauer's arm moved in automated response.

He stopped, mind racing.

'Hitler is dead, my friend.'

'The man is dead; the movement lives.'

Bauer nodded, mesmerised by glacier-blue eyes glistening with conviction. Who was this beanpole? He had to be mad.

'Why me?'

'Gestapo. Not the same calibre as SS, but good enough.' Chin upturned; eyes narrowed in imagined triumph.

'How did you know?'

'Everyone knows. It's tattooed on our souls. This – he pointed to the jagged double S on his underarm – this is just a symbol.'

Bauer nodded again.

'And the plan?'

'I shall be in touch. First, we need to find out the numbers. Who's left. Who's unbroken. Then we plan. Heil Hitler.'

'Wait, I have questions.'

Too late; the man headed off. Bauer leaned against a rough trunk as his stalker disappeared into the trees. A few seconds later, there was no trace of him. You had to admire skill like that, even if the man stood for everything he hated. So why this strange feeling of relief that radiated through him like a hot shower after a winter's drenching? Perhaps he wanted to be caught; stop running; come out of hiding; receive orders and obey them.

He stumbled back down to the farm. Would this hell never end? This wasn't what he wanted. Why hadn't he told him as much? What on earth possessed him to ask about a plan? The war was over, wasn't it? Why couldn't he live in peace with his family?

Anger bubbled up inside him, a witch's cauldron of missed opportunities, guilt, and fear. Just when he thought he was getting his head above the stinking soup, someone, something, pushed him down under again.

Head bowed, shoulders slack, he trudged by the hay barn. A sudden movement startled him. It was Wanda; she gave a little wave before turning inside the barn's dark interior. Was she watching him? Had she seen him meet his SS stalker? Had she engineered it herself? But how? No, he was being ridiculous. Or was he? What did he really know about this woman who had become part of his household? Befriended by his wife, her position was unassailable; the thought scraped his skull like a fingernail on slate.

The sun was starting its slow descent as he sank down on the bench outside the kitchen door and removed his cracked boots before stepping inside. His wife was kneading dough; the brown mass spread and came together in a soothing dance across the floured table.

'We need to talk, Henni.'

'Not now, Heinz.'

This was what their marriage had descended to: a litany of not now, later, can't you see I'm busy. Yet theirs had been a good marriage for so many years. She had always deferred to him, but he had never abused his position as head of the family. He listened; he took her views and comments on board so that the decisions seemed made together; at least to him they did.

Now, she was in charge; had been since the day of the row, which threatened to blast them apart.

He slumped in the comfortable red leather armchair belonging to his father-in-law, Gunter, and closed his eyes. The slow shuffle of slippered feet across the stone floor intruded on his thoughts.

'Gunter?' A bony hand reached for his.

'No, Lottie, it's me, Heinz. Gunter is still out tending to the cows.' His voice was tender as he smiled at his children's grandmother, their beloved Oma. Was Henni paying any attention? No, she was still busy kneading and didn't look up.

Lottie's mind was disintegrating; her periods of lucidity were rare, and she no longer functioned at the centre of the home. So, his wife had taken over the shopping, cooking, cleaning, and farm accounts.

'Would you like to sit down?'

She shook her head and wandered off.

'Can you keep an eye on her? I'm about to start cooking and I don't want her near the range.'

It was all he was good for these days, baby-sitting her mother when he wasn't working in the fields.

'Lottie? Come and play cards with me.'

Heinz set up a small card table next to his chair and started shuffling a pack of cards. Lottie's eyes lit up with pleasure. She wasn't capable of playing rummy anymore, always her favourite game, but seemed to find shuffling and laying out the cards for a game of patience absorbing.

Heinz would talk to her the entire time, explaining his thought processes as he reached for the cards. He never finished a game because she would pick up random cards and examine them or hold them to her chest and refuse to give them back.

'That's why it's called patience, Lottie.' Her opaque eyes searched his. What did she see? What did she understand about her condition? Or the world outside their farm? She giggled and shook her finger at him.

'Naughty Gunter.'

He didn't contradict her. As long as she sat beside him, he was doing his job and free to contemplate his bizarre meeting in the forest.

The movement lives, his pursuer had said. What did he mean? How could there be any movement with Hitler dead? He was the maniac who had led them into this mess. Without him, there was nothing, surely? Germany had surrendered unconditionally on May 7th. The Allies had divided the country, and he knew he was lucky to be in the American zone; they were all lucky, especially his wife and daughters.

The ten of clubs morphed into a photograph of murdered children. He shook his head to rid himself of the image. He remembered all too clearly the cold mist-laden October evening he had heard about Nemmersdorf, a village in East Prussia taken by Soviet troops before the Wehrmacht beat them back.

Henni had already returned to her family's farm in Bavaria, together with their three children, leaving him in Krakow. It was a Friday, and he had finished work early. He was on his way home, wondering whether to reheat some leftover stew or dine out. Managing on his own wasn't a problem, but he missed his family and bought a newspaper to occupy his thoughts as he ate alone. What he read killed his appetite.

Under the headline "The Raving of Soviet Beasts" glared the photograph of murdered children; bile rasped his throat as he scanned the reports of plunder and destruction, murder and rape. The Volkischer Beobachter was the main Nazi newspaper, but there was nothing triumphalist about its tone now just dire warnings that the villagers' fate awaited every German who did not fight to the bitter end. He swallowed hard. He thought of his wife and children. This could have happened to them, to his beloved family. It's what every reader would be thinking as they determined whether to battle on.

When he returned to work, Nemmersdorf was tight on everyone's lips. His secretary, Brigitta, kept shaking her head and he noticed all the women whispering together at every opportunity. They gathered by the wooden filing cabinets, clung to each other in corridors, disappeared into the toilets. They were like skittish roe deer sensing the presence of wolves but too frightened to scatter in the wrong direction. He had every sympathy for them. The Soviets had been in Poland since the early days of the war; if the Allies won the war, as seemed likely, it would be the Bolshevik hoards who overran Krakow.

'They say they crucified some of the villagers.'

'Now, Brigitta, it doesn't do to believe everything you read in the papers. The essential truth is there, of course, but some of our journalists can get carried away in their fervour for the Fatherland and our beloved Fuehrer.'

Did that strike the right tone? Comfort mixed with loyalty. Never forget to demonstrate loyalty to the Fuehrer. They could still send him to the Eastern front, after all.

She was chewing her bottom lip, her eyes unfocused and large with horror. Her white blouse looked crumpled as if she'd slept in it. He wanted to put his arm around her, reassure her, maybe send her away from the horrors to come.

'Where is home?'

'Home?' She looked at him, taken aback by the question.

'I mean, where are your folks? Where do you come from?'

'Stuttgart.'

'And is all well with your family there?'

'Yes, yes, thank you.'

'That's good, Brigitta. You know if things get difficult here, I can always arrange for you to visit them.'

Her eyes welled up; her lips moved towards a smile.

'Thank you, Inspector Bauer.'

'No need. However, I would be very grateful for a coffee.'

'Of course. It's on its way.'

He wondered where she was now. He didn't suppose he would ever find out.

The door to the farmhouse swung open, and the kitchen filled with the joyous chatter of his six-year-old son, Tomas.

'Papa, Papa, I milked Brunhilda today, didn't I, Opa?'

Tomas clambered onto his father's lap and started playing with the buttons on his shirt, stretching his hand out to touch two at once.

'You did, my boy. You did very well.'

Gunter nodded at Heinz, but his eyes darted this way and that, and he strode off to wash his hands. At the sink he rubbed his daughter's back; she turned and placed her head against his shoulder for a moment.

His body tensed at the tender scene which no

longer encompassed him. Anger threatened to crush the diamond jack in his hand. What the hell had happened? How had he fallen outside their affectionate embrace? Did the years of unity mean nothing? Was he no longer a member of this family?

'Papa, you're not listening.'

'You're right, little man. My thoughts distracted me. Now tell me all about Brunhilda. Did she kick you?'

'No, Papa.' The outraged voice made Heinz smile, and he ruffled his son's hair.

'Well, she kicked me when I tried to milk her'.

'Did she? Did you tickle her? She doesn't like being tickled. You must use firm hands and a firm stroke, and she likes it best when you sing to her.'

'Does she? Nobody told me that. So, what did you sing to her?'

'I made up a song. Do you want to hear it?'

'Yes, please, that would be wonderful.'

'It goes: Brunhilda, Brunhilda, we call all cows that are brown Brunhilda. Brun, Brun, Brun, Brun, Hilda, Hilda, Hilda, Hilda.'

Heinz resisted an urge to grin at the reedy voice.

'And she likes that song?'

'Yes, she does.'

'I shall have to remember that if I ever have to milk her again.'

'Don't worry, Papa, I can always help you.'

'Thank you, Tomas. Now, I think you may need to wash your hands ready for supper.'

Heinz lifted his son down onto the floor. Wanda was laying the table. As usual, she had come inside unnoticed.

Her ability to glide into place whenever Henni needed her gave him the creeps. She was like a ghost moving through walls.

Lottie had fallen asleep, her mouth drooling; a bubbly thread of saliva slithered down between the hairs on her chin. He reached for the card that had slipped out of her hand and strayed into the folds of her housecoat. She moaned, woke up with a start, and screamed at him repeatedly. It was a pathetic sound, like the screech of a wounded bird. The gaping hole, the shaking body, the eyes narrowing with every scream rooted him to the spot. When he didn't react, she started flailing his chest with her puny arms.

Gunter rushed forward, enfolded her in his embrace, and rocked her back and forth, whispering to her until she calmed down and lay sobbing; eventually, her clenched fists softened, and the outburst was over.

Heinz gathered the cards, fumbling and dropping them before shoving them into a wooden box, carved and painted with the four suits. Cheeks flushed, he busied himself putting the box away, unable to look anybody in the face. He stared daggers at Lottie. Would his demented cry have attracted their sympathy? Or would they have just ignored him like they did now? He was behaving like a child but knowing that didn't seem to make any difference. He kicked the card table shut and vowed never to play again. His stomach hardened as he thought how unfair it all was. He should have refused to look after her; that's what he would do next time. He'd show them how much they needed him.

The screaming had fetched his two daughters,

Monika and Carola, downstairs, and now they held each of Lottie's hands and guided her to the table. Sullen faced, he dragged leaden feet to join them. Eight sat around the beech trestle table made by Gunter's grandfather from a storm-damaged tree: Gunter at the head of the table; the children on a bench down one side together with Wanda; Lottie and his wife facing them and Heinz at the far end, opposite Gunter.

They tucked into steaming bowls of thick green soup. Tiny fragments of bacon fat glistened on the surface, teasing their nostrils with the promise of meat. He dreamt of bacon: the fat turned to crisp; perhaps they all did. Not that they lacked meat; rabbit stew featured regularly, as did breaded rabbit cutlets. Monotonous, yes, but wholesome, nutritious food that filled their bellies and let his children thrive.

'There's bread and cheese to follow, but the next loaf will be our last for a while,' said Henni. 'I've used up our stores of flour and I haven't seen any on sale for months now.'

'You've done well, Henni. We'll manage fine without, but I'll put the word out in case any of our neighbours can help. I remember Hans saying he was going to experiment with Spring wheat. It's worth asking him.'

Henni smiled at her father. Heinz winced; he should have been the one to praise his wife and appreciate her efforts. Even when they had lived in Berlin, she had been a brilliant housekeeper, but here in the countryside she knew and loved there was no end to her talents. By the end of Autumn, she had filled the larder with jars of vegetables, some salted, some pickled; dried yellow and black mushrooms hung from hooks like misshapen necklaces; jars of golden honey, some with waxy combs, promised tastes of summer richness; there were sweet-smelling apples in the attic; plump pumpkins and squashes sat on shelves in the hay barn, hidden from a casual glance by mounds of loose hay; root vegetables nestled in damp sand in clamps under the lean-to.

Now that Spring was upon them, the garden would yield fresh delights supplemented by her careful foraging for young nettles and pungent handfuls of wild garlic. It had amazed him on their walks in Berlin, when they still talked, how she would pick weeds in the park to supplement their own diet. She'd teased him about being a townie.

'How on earth would you survive without me?'

'I wouldn't want to.'

He missed their easy-going, loving relationship more than he could bear. Perhaps his forest stalker could help? Heinz imagined himself negotiating a sack of flour for his cooperation in whatever plan was being concocted and returning home triumphant, the family provider of old. Would Henni look at him with love in her eyes again? Would she whisper how proud she was of him, of everything he had done and continued to do for his family?

His back straightened and he shifted on his seat. There was always plenty to do around the farm and he knew he pulled his weight. He wasn't keen on milking the cows, but he had mechanical skills and plenty of muscle power. The farm would have been far less productive without him. He didn't need his stalker to justify his existence, but remembering those piercing eyes he had to admit there was something exciting about him.

'Mama, may we get down from the table?'

She used to make them wait until Wanda had finished eating, but the children were so frustrated by the interminable wait that Henni had relented months ago; if the other adults had finished, they could go and play. The men moved across to their chairs by the fireplace.

'A glass of Schnapps, Heinz?'

Gunter reached for the bottle and a couple of glasses stored on the shelves above a small writing desk.

'That must have been a shock for you today,' he said, pouring out a generous measure. 'Down it in one and I'll fill you up again.'

Heinz didn't argue and closed his eyes as the spicy warmth spread through his chest. Wait. How did he know? Gunter had been busy with the cows and would never have left Tomas on his own to follow him into the forest. He said nothing and waited.

Gunter refilled both their glasses and sighed.

'When the doctor warned us to expect episodes like that one, I must admit I didn't believe him,' he said.

'Lottie has always been so gentle. She brought up four boys in addition to Henni, and she never had to smack them or even raise her voice. Bringing up boys can cause a real tussle of wills. I've seen it in other families, but Lottie just had a way about her. Beats me what the secret is. I used to get annoyed with them and would have to walk away and leave Lottie to it. And now this. I think at some level she recognises her brain is going and she must feel so frustrated by it. I'm sorry, Heinz.'

'You have nothing to apologise for. It was a shock because it was so unexpected, but she didn't hurt me or anything. And now I'll be more prepared for it, if it happens again.'

They sat, sipping their drinks. Heinz longed to share his forest encounter with his father-in-law. Some instinct stopped him. He was certain Gunter would not approve of any resurgence of National Socialism. He also knew that information was power, and he needed to hold on to any vestige in this strange world.

The photograph of Gunter's youngest son, Albrecht, dressed in his SS uniform was nowhere to be seen now. But then you would expect that. No point flagging up his existence to any visiting Allied soldiers.

Heinz had never liked the man; bumptious prig sprang to mind. He had been an early recruit to the National Socialist Party and eager to do his bit to make Germany glorious again. That included a determination to recruit his new brother-in-law and lecture him on the Fuehrer's wisdom which seemed to involve blaming the Jews for everything. He was also tall, well built, with the Aryan ideal of blue eyes and fair hair. But where others admired a Nazi pin-up boy, Heinz saw only an icy stare, a cruel mouth, and a humourless expression. He wasn't surprised when Albrecht joined the SS, Hitler's elite forces. He'll go far, he had thought, and he was right. By 1940, still in his twenties, he was already a Captain based in Krakow, the capital of the General Government zone of occupation in Poland.

And yet, without Albrecht, he would now be a Russian prisoner of war. Or dead.

CHAPTER 2

SPADE HIT GROUND IN a steady rhythm: Heinz was digging over a fresh patch of land to extend the vegetable garden. Hard physical labour suited his mood. He could break the soil even if he couldn't break through to his wife. He might as well be a hermit for all the comfort he derived from married life. Isolation had seeped into his bones; his skull formed the bars of a cage, keeping him locked in melancholy. Death played on his mind; the prospect of eternal sleep gave him a frisson of pleasure. She'd be sorry then; he cringed and spat on the ground; the bitter taste remained in his mouth.

How long was it since his encounter in the forest? He tried counting back the days, but they all merged into one. Only the peal of church bells calling people to redemption signalled the week's end. Like a prisoner, he had taken to marking the calendar, but to no avail. Monday, Thursday, what difference did it make?

The stalker was his distraction. Now he was glad he'd kept quiet: it was his secret, his opportunity to escape the banality of his life in hiding. He looked forward to seeing him again, even though he was a link to the past he was trying to forget.

Whenever the farm's guard dogs started barking and

straining at their chains, he would run for cover. When he first hunkered down on the farm, he feared Nazi hunters looking for deserters; now he was more concerned about Allied troops seeking revenge for the war. He had a hideaway inside the house, though he didn't hold out much hope of its resilience to a systematic search. Hadn't he broken down doors, ripped up floorboards, tested walls for cavities as a Gestapo officer searching for members of the resistance? Not his own work, of course, but directed by him. He was an expert at it; he relied on his sixth sense to find them. There was no pleasure in it; a nasty fate awaited them, whether during interrogation or afterwards. But he had a family to look after and this was war, justified or not.

He and Gunter had also built a den in the forest. They had camouflaged it well, and he had practised running to it. It was of limited use against determined men with tracker dogs, or his solitary stalker for that matter, but it was somewhere to hide during a routine inspection of the farm and would give him time to plan an escape. Perhaps that's what he needed to do now? Escape and let Henni enjoy her freedom from him? The family would be all right; nobody was interested in persecuting women and children. But what would he do? Where would he go?

He stopped for a break. A light marked a small circle on the leather jerkin he'd hung over the fence. A brighter day and he would never have spotted it. It flashed on and off. He counted one, two, three, four. A break. Then it started again. One, two, three, four. Morse code for HH. Heil Hitler, what else could it be? He was back.

Heinz lifted his spade in both hands, pretending to stretch his muscles. He checked the surroundings. The dogs were quiet. There was nobody around. He struck the spade into the ground, threw on his jerkin, and loped towards the forest, just like a hunting dog himself.

'Let's go to your den.'

'You've discovered my bolthole?'

He smiled and shrugged his shoulders. 'It's part of the job.'

Heinz followed, awed by his abilities. Imagine having a deputy like that. He grimaced; more likely he would have been the deputy. They sat down in the mossy den, breathing in the smell of ancient soil mixed with the resinous fragrance of spruce. Heinz reached into the corner, dug around, and pulled out two bottles. He wiped them clean and handed one over.

'Ah, I didn't spot those.'

'I suppose not, or they wouldn't be here.'

'I don't steal from brother officers.'

'Who do you steal from?'

'Our oppressors.'

Heinz choked on his beer. Oppression? Well, he would know all about that in the SS, men notorious for their cruelty to the enemy.

'I'm not used to this stuff anymore,' he said, reaching out his hand. 'Heinz Bauer, as I'm sure I don't need to tell you.'

'Alp. That's all.' But he shook hands with a warmth belying his nickname.

'Do you have any food? To go with the beer?'

Bauer had suspected his rat-like features resulted

from hunger as much as hereditary bone structure. He reached into his jerkin and pulled out his mid-morning snack, a hunk of cheese wrapped in cloth.

'Thanks.'

'So, what can you tell me?'

Alp was munching on the cheese, eyes like shards of ice locked into Bauer's. The silence continued as Bauer sipped on his beer. Was it a test? He relaxed and leaned back against the banked soil; he wasn't in any hurry to return to his spade.

'What do you know about Operation Werewolf?'

Of course. He should have realised. Work on the farm had pulped his brain. He studied a wood beetle making its way around the tip of his foot; rubbed the back of his neck; felt a tightness in his chest. He didn't know what was worse: his lack of insight or dealing with a fantasist. With a raised eyebrow, he turned to Alp and howled.

'My werewolf teeth bite... hoo, hoo, hoo.' In a falsetto voice, he mimicked the propaganda broadcasts from Radio Werewolf.

'I see you are not a genuine believer.' His voice was stinging, eyes flints.

Bauer gripped his beer tight. Thoughts buzzed around his brain like a furious wasp trapped in a jar. Fear jiggered his nerves and sent his heartbeat racing. It was foolish to insult Alp, make a joke of it, mock a fanatic. He had angered a potential foe. Would he pull a gun on him? Would he die here in the forest? Death to the unbeliever. Would Henni even care? He licked his lips; his voice came as a whisper.

'It seems such an impossible task.'

Alp leant forward, rushing at his words.

'No, no, no. You haven't seen what I've seen. It would inspire you, Bauer, truly it would.'

His eyes glowed, unblinking.

'Conquer or die. What could be more beautiful, more honourable? They planned all this. Think about it: the very name his parents gave him, Adolf, means both noble and wolf. It was his destiny and Hitler never shied from referring to himself as Wolf or to his Wolf's Lair.'

Bauer sat rock-like. What a ridiculous motto for a defeated nation. Conquer or die when they were already conquered and half-dead.

'Look, I can guess what you're thinking: Wolf is dead. That's it, isn't it? You can't see it working because our beloved Fuehrer is no longer here to give us the lead, give us his inspiration, his strength.'

'Something like that.'

'I was there at the start of Operation Werewolf. Skorzeny himself handpicked me. My God, there was an inspiring man. Imagine it: one day you're sitting at a desk job in Berlin, bits of shrapnel still in the back of your head and an Iron Cross around your neck and the next you're leading an audacious mission to rescue Mussolini from a prison high in the Apennine Mountains. "I knew my friend Adolf wouldn't desert me." That's what he said to old Scarface when he rescued him. And not a single shot fired throughout the mission.'

But another maniac leader dead, thought Bauer. Shot by firing squad and strung up for all to mock.

'I don't deny it's a blow that Hitler's dead. Some of

the younger Werewolves still can't accept it. They say he must have escaped, that the Russians never produced his body, that he's out there somewhere. They're wrong, of course, but you can understand why grief muddles up their thinking. No, Hitler always said death was preferable to defeat. We're all prepared to die, but first, we have work to accomplish.'

'Which is what exactly?'

'Well, the guerrilla operations continue as before: harass the enemy; shoot the collaborators; destroy supply lines; keep the Allied bastards permanently on their toes so they can never enjoy the fruits of victory because victory without its fruits is no victory at all.'

'And you have the manpower? The weapons?'

'We've trained thousands, both SS and Hitler Youth. Don't forget Operation Werewolf started in late summer, maybe early autumn last year, well before Goebbels got in on the act. I'm not saying he didn't help, but we already had an elite force of young men and soldiers ready to intimidate the enemy.'

'And the weapons?'

'Oh, don't you worry about the weapons. Our training was as thorough as you would expect of the Third Reich. Every Werewolf knows how to produce explosives from household objects; each recruit can strangle a man in one swift movement.'

Bauer didn't doubt it. He shivered, imagining Alp's slender fingers tightening on a cord around his own neck. There was a dangerous undertone to everything Alp said: participation in his activities was only partially voluntary.

'Even so, you want more than home-grown basics to fight a guerrilla war.'

Long minutes passed before Alp responded.

'I suppose there's no harm in telling you. Weapons can be a problem. We've had a bit of a setback here in Bavaria recently. The Allies captured one of our cells hiding out in a tunnel network in Schönsee at the end of April. Six officers and 25 men were taken prisoner as well as weapons, ammunition, explosives, communications equipment, and several months' worth of food supplies. They also found a couple of vehicles hidden in the nearby forest.

'Mm, that's a blow.'

'An irritation.'

'Why do I feel you're not telling me something?'

Alp grinned, revealing a snaggle-tooth. 'They told me you relied on your instincts. They weren't wrong, were they?'

'Who's they?'

'Never mind. The point is, will you help us?'

'I need more time to think. I want to understand the full picture before I commit myself.'

'That's reasonable. At the same time, I must protect my organisation. I need to be sure of you. Then I can reveal any other details.'

'That makes sense.'

They clinked bottles and downed the last of the beer before setting off in separate directions. After a few steps, Bauer looked over his shoulder. Alp was nowhere to be seen.

He chuckled and with a sudden rush of energy ran

down the hill to the farm, prompting an outburst of frenzied barking from the guard dogs. He slowed to a walking pace and was about to whistle the special tune to reassure them he wasn't a danger when he stopped dead.

Standing at the kitchen door, pointing a shotgun straight at him, was Henni.

Christ, he didn't know this woman at all. She whistled at the dogs, and they fell silent.

'Where the hell have you been?'

'At the den. I thought…'

'The dogs never barked.'

'No, but I saw something. The scent wouldn't have reached the dogs. How did you know I'd gone?'

'I came to bring you a coffee mid-morning.'

His eyes softened. How long had it been since she'd made any sort of gesture towards him? Any act of kindness?

'Thank you. That was thoughtful of you. Are you going to put that down? Do you even know how to use it?'

Henni pushed the catch and broke the gun with practised ease.

'I know how to use it, all right. Stay out of the kitchen. I've just washed the floor.'

With that, she disappeared behind the door. The moment was lost and another opportunity to talk denied him. He considered ignoring her instruction, barging into the kitchen, grabbing her by the shoulders, and demanding they get to the bottom of this deadlock in their relationship; it wouldn't work, not in her domain. The circumstances needed to be more auspicious.

He stomped towards the kitchen garden, threw his jerkin at the fence, and slammed the spade into the ground, where it hit a root and rebounded on him. He winced and launched the spade into the air, glaring as it landed among the trees.

'That was stupid. You could have broken the shaft.'

He whipped around. Wanda stood at the garden gate, hoe in hand, biting her lips to suppress a smile. Was she flirting with him? She wore a blue flowered dress Heinz vaguely remembered seeing Henni wear during their courtship. It contoured her breasts and hips and forced the realisation on him that she had filled out into an attractive woman. A very attractive woman.

He stroked his throat and suppressed a moan. As if he needed any complications in his life? He closed his eyes and breathed in the scent of fresh growth, a hint of mint, a scattering of apple blossom, and the faintly arousing smell of newly bathed skin.

'Why are you still here, Wanda?'

She shrugged, moved inside the garden, and closed the gate with a playful shove.

'The food is plentiful and good. Besides...'

'Besides?'

'It suits me to be amongst damaged people.'

He felt giddy. The world darkened; he was going to faint. Deep, calming breaths steadied his nerves as he focused on Wanda's retreating back. What the hell did she mean? Damaged people indeed. The cheek of it. And yet, the words stayed with him as he dug into the ground, as he rested, as he freshened himself up, as he sat down to the evening meal. He watched all of them through her eyes: Lottie babbling away to herself; Gunter with his sad eyes and head bowed; Henni endlessly busy, snapping at the slightest provocation.

'Tomas! If you slurp your soup like a pig, you'll go to your room with no supper.'

Where the hell had that come from? She'd always insisted on good manners, at the table and elsewhere, but her reaction seemed unnecessarily harsh. His sweet little son was now too frightened to move, let alone eat, biting back the tears. Monika sat aloof at the end of the bench. Carola looked tearful in sympathy with her brother. And how did he appear? Lonely? Angry? Confused? Lost?

He'd felt all of these since his return to the farm. As long as his marriage had been solid, he'd forged a path between superficial loyalty to the regime and subversive actions designed to help people escape its brutality. Not too many, of course; he wasn't a saint. He needed to survive and protect his family by remaining above suspicion. He wasn't proud of the role he'd played in Hitler's Germany, but it could have been worse; he could have been worse; he could have become a cold-blooded Nazi especially when he moved across to the Gestapo and he didn't. That was worth something, surely?

Now the war was over, and he was drowning. Was Henni disappointed in him? Did she think he should have stayed in Krakow? Did she despise his balancing act, neither one thing nor the other? How could he find out if they never talked? How ironic that Hitler's death had ended communication between them. Was it the same for other couples? Throughout the Nazi stranglehold on their country, they had watched their tongues because they never knew who was listening, who was ready to denounce them. And yet, they understood each other; they felt close and managed to communicate in their own way. This new silence between them was like a thick prison wall.

He thought of Alp and an agreeable shiver tickled his spine. He had sparked something deep inside him: camaraderie, a sense of belonging. The SS officer accepted him and that made him feel good about himself, he didn't deny it. Of course, Alp assumed he'd been a diligent Nazi and he wasn't about to disabuse him. Could he play the man the way he'd played his bosses during the war? Maintain interest but stall any activities? Guerrilla warfare didn't interest him in the slightest, but being part of something again, oh yes, that appealed enormously.

What a mess it all was; what a mess he was. Wanda, still sitting at the table, was slowly chewing her food. She had every right to be damaged and yet, just then, she seemed the strongest of them all.

CHAPTER 3

THAT NIGHT, SLEEP ELUDED him. Tomas had woken early with a bad tummy and Henni had stopped the night in his bedroom; at least Heinz wasn't disturbing her. He tossed and turned, pummelled the pillows, sat on the edge of the bed, walked around the room. It was too hot, then too cold. He switched on the light and checked the time: 2am. Creeping downstairs, he drank a glass of water and made himself comfortable.

The house settled itself around him: odd creaks and sighs from floorboards or walls felt reassuring. He went to the bookshelf and picked out the family encyclopaedia. It was a large, red-bound book with gold lettering on a black spine. He flicked through the pages looking for German folklore. Under the entry for Alp, he found a gruesome illustration of the demon. The creature was male and attacked women during the night sitting astride their chests and crushing them.

Alp was best known for his ability to change appearance, most often into a cat, dog, pig or snake. Heinz remembered the way Alp disappeared into the forest. He smirked, perhaps he could just as easily turn himself into a fir or spruce? The demon proper always wore a hat known as a Tankappe which gave him magical powers. He also possessed an evil eye whose gaze could inflict illness and misfortune. Heinz had no doubt his Alp could do the same, with or without the muzzle of a gun.

Heinz had never taken much notice of the Nazi obsession with the supernatural. He wasn't interested in religion, let alone magic, but it was strange the way these ideas persisted. He remembered Albrecht boasting about his visit to Himmler's castle at Wewelsburg. Decorated like a medieval knightly court, it had its own Merlin, an elderly sage who claimed to be descended from the gods and held his audience spellbound with stories of telepathic deities and ancestral white supermen. Drug-inspired nonsense, he had always thought privately; it didn't do to voice these opinions out loud, not if you wanted to survive the war. And he had survived it. The question was how was he going to survive the peace?

Six months had now passed since his boss, Criminal Director Fuchs, had left his office ashen-faced and ordered – no, that was the wrong word – suggested, perhaps, that he made himself known to the occupant. Heinz had knocked, entered, and executed the Heil Hitler salute as his brother-in-law, Albrecht Hoffman, now a Lieutenant-Colonel, sat watching him, hands steepled in front of his face, legs stretched out across the corner of the desk.

'Sit down, Bauer.'

He did as he was told.

'I've told Fuchs you're going to carry out a mission for me.'

Bauer cocked his head to one side.

'Oh, don't worry, he won't interfere. Stupid man thinks I don't know what he's been up to these last few years. Well, I've given him some food for thought there. Enough to spoil his appetite for good, the gluttonous slob. I want you to drive Magda and the children to my parents' farm. They're to stop there until I join them in due course. You'll have a Mercedes truck with sufficient fuel to get you there and back. And mind you do come back. I won't tolerate any desertion, any disloyalty to our Fuehrer or to our cause.'

Bauer nodded. 'Of course. I understand.'

'Mind you do. I won't have the slightest hesitation in tracking you down and shooting you myself if you disobey my orders.'

'Yes, Sir.'

'We will come on a family visit to your apartment this Sunday. The children and Magda will remain with you. I've ordered the truck with their luggage and additional fuel to be delivered to you early Monday morning and you will set off immediately. These passes – he pushed an envelope across the desk – will ensure your uninterrupted passage to the farm. You will also have these funds – another envelope appeared – to do as you see fit in any emergencies.

'The truck is equipped with snow chains and a shovel in case the weather changes for the worse. You can never tell in Bavaria. Oh, and there's a basic toolbox. I'm assuming you can carry out minor repairs if the occasion arises, although it's been given a thorough service, so I don't expect any problems.

'There will be bedding in the back in case of any

holdups. It'll make the journey more comfortable for Magda, as well as the children. She's not been herself since the last pregnancy ended so unfortunately.'

'Sir?'

'I suppose there's no reason you should know. Magda gave birth prematurely in October. All the Russian rumours didn't help, I imagine. Anyway, the sickly mite only survived a few days. Long enough to ensure a gold medal for her child-bearing efforts, but her body still hasn't recovered.'

Bauer swallowed hard. How could he talk about medals when his own flesh and blood had died? The man was a monster.

'The exact nature of the mission will remain secret, though I don't suppose Fuchs will dare ask you about it. Is that understood?'

'Yes, Sir.'

'That includes contacting Henni or anyone else.'

'Understood.'

'You have a Walther PPK, I assume.'

'Yes, Sir.'

'I have ordered Fuchs to give you another gun and several boxes of ammunition. Make sure you get those. We're getting increasing reports of lawlessness around the country: foreign workers flexing their muscles in the light of Allied advances. We've got contingency plans to deal with any large-scale uprising, but it's best to be prepared for every eventuality. These are dangerous times, Bauer, so don't hesitate to shoot the bastards if you come across them.

'Now, is there anything else you need to know?'

'No, I don't think so.'

'Good. I will see you on Sunday.'

After Albrecht Hoffman had left the room, Bauer looked out the window, imagining the joy of his reunion with Henni and the children. How many months had it been? He leant against the frame and closed his eyes. To hold his precious wife in his arms again would be bliss, even if his stay had to be short. He glanced through the envelopes Hoffman had given him: the money was substantial; if he didn't use all of it perhaps he could leave some with Henni to help her out. There were two passes, signed and stamped by Hoffman, for himself and for Magda and the children. They specified a route from Krakow to Bavaria but made no mention of a return journey for Bauer. It seemed odd; maybe you only needed passes to leave the Central Government in case you were running away whereas coming back you would be welcomed with open arms. No doubt Hoffman knew what he was doing.

Bauer spent the remaining two days making lists, rearranging his diary, writing up reports, and leaving instructions for his secretary. On Saturday he shopped, buying any provisions he could get for the journey and little gifts for Henni and the children. That night, he picked at his food, impatient to be on his way. He woke early on Sunday and packed a small bag for himself. On an impulse, he repacked his stuff into a haversack and found his blackthorn hiking stick, an early present from Henni.

He had always loved hiking in the Bavarian mountains; it was there he had first met Henni and fallen in love. When this war was over, they'd go back to their favourite haunts and introduce their children to the joys of hiking. It would be fun; it would be normal; they would be a proper family again. He spent most of the day waiting. Albrecht had given him no indication of time, so he found himself constantly pricking his ears for a knock at the door or checking the window for any signs of his passengers. By late afternoon, he began to fear that something had gone wrong with the mission; perhaps the whole trip would be called off; with a pounding heart, he pictured Albrecht telling him to return to work on Monday.

Then, at six o'clock, they arrived. Albrecht entered the apartment first, carrying one of his younger daughters and holding a small boy by the hand. Magda, long hair braided around her head like a helmet, followed him, ushering in four children of various heights. Finally, a young woman carrying a sleeping toddler slipped in behind them and melted into the background.

'Welcome, welcome,' said Bauer with a warm smile, fussing over the children as if they were his own, chucking chins and ruffling hair. Solemn eyes stared up at him; none of them spoke.

'The children have had an early supper so they can be put to bed immediately. Show her where to go, Bauer.' Albrecht jerked his head in the direction of the woman whose eyes never left the ground but seemed to know she was being called forth.

'This way,' said Bauer, opening the bedroom doors off the main corridor. 'I'll sleep on the sofa so you can use the double bed and the children's beds.'

Both women followed him, and Magda started allocating the rooms. Bauer rejoined his brother-in-law and offered him a Schnapps while they waited. He refused and pulled out a silver hip flask. A delicate aroma wafted across the room. Brandy? Cognac? What refined tastes he had developed since leaving the farm.

'Magda said she couldn't manage without the nanny, so you've got an extra passenger. Here's an extra pass just in case anyone decides to bother about her.'

Bauer nodded acceptance as he took the pass and then downed his drink.

'The truck will be here at 7am. I will expect you to be gone by half past.'

'Will you say goodnight to the children?' Magda put her head around the door.

'No need. I'll be off now.'

Magda ran to her husband, and he kissed her. Bauer turned away, startled by the vehemence of their embrace. Of almost equal height, they towered over him like a marital fortress, one that didn't include children it seemed.

Once they were alone, Bauer offered her a Schnapps. She stared at the bottle in his hand and shook her head without conviction.

'Perhaps just a small one? To help you relax in a strange apartment and ahead of a long journey?' He took her silence for acquiescence and poured her a measure equal to his own.

'Bavaria, here we come.' She greeted the toast in silence. Not long after, Magda took herself off to bed and he was left picking at the plates of meat and cheese he had prepared earlier, never imagining their journey would backfire so spectacularly in ways he barely understood, even now.

Gunter's grandfather clock chimed the hour: 3am. He shivered and wrapped his dressing gown tighter around his body. He ought to go to bed, though its single occupancy held no attraction. More and more, he wondered if the key to his unhappiness lay in their unexpected arrival at the farm. Albrecht had insisted on secrecy, but shock is never a good tactic in family relationships.

It was late in the afternoon and raining hard when they pulled up outside the farmhouse. After a mostly uneventful journey lasting two tiring days, they encountered bedlam: dogs barking; his children shrieking in delight; the Hoffman brood chattering in equal delight; the toddler screaming and straining to be put down; Lottie crooning to herself and dancing around the kitchen; Gunter bewildered and Henni stony-faced.

'You'd better explain what this is all about?' Her tone was sharp, unforgiving. Had they even embraced each other? He didn't think so.

The children disappeared upstairs while the toddler was kept amused by the nanny. As he related his mission, Henni prepared tea and slapped food on the table. Bread and butter, cheeses, pickles, cakes and biscuits. She kept glancing at the nanny and toddler, and he remembered thinking that she must be mourning their own baby, Lisle, who would have been at a similar age if she had survived.

'Sit down, please, all of you,' said Henni, her voice straining to remain polite.

'Shall I call the children?' asked Gunter.

'No, they'll appear soon enough if they're hungry.' Henni moved across to the nanny, took the child from her arms, and indicated the table.

'She doesn't eat with us,' said Magda, scorn infecting every word.

'She does in this house.'

'No, no, no. I won't allow it.' Magda rose from her seat, towering above all of them. The screech of her voice made Lottie whimper and hide her face in the crook of Gunter's arm.

'This is my house,' said Henni, her eyes narrowed to slits, 'And my rules and you will not treat any human being the way you have treated her and no doubt many others.'

The colour drained from Magda's face, and she sank back down.

'That is preposterous. I can't stay here if you insist on treating criminals like members of the family.'

'You're quite right, Magda. You can't stay here, and you won't. As soon as you've eaten something, you'll be on your way to your own family home.'

'What? You can't do that.'

'I most certainly can.'

'Henni?' Gunter intervened; his tone uncertain.

'No, Papa, I can't bear it. I simply can't bear it.'

And that was the end of the discussion. Heinz had difficulty remembering the rest of the meal in any detail: at some point the children joined them; Magda sulked and muttered about Albrecht; Gunter produced a map showing the best route to her village; he tried to calculate distances and fuel requirements; Henni sat next to the nanny and made a point of talking to her with her back turned to the others. She left the table at one point and loaded a variety of provisions into a battered wicker basket, which Gunter carried outside and must have loaded into the truck. She ordered their resentful children to bed, and they came and hugged their father, trying to prolong their stay with their cousins.

Then came the unforgettable finale. Magda organised her children into the truck, settled the now sleeping toddler and returned, shaking with fury. She advanced on Henni with finger pointed, eyes blazing, and voice carved with icy precision.

'Do not think you can get away with this. Albrecht is the man of this house, not you.'

At this point, Gunther, with a quiet dignity befitting his advanced years, corrected his daughter-in-law.

'Actually, I am still the head of this house, and I shall remain so until I die.'

'Of course, Gunter, I only meant that Henni has no right to usurp her brother's authority. Albrecht planned this for all our benefits and it's ludicrous to let her sympathies for a criminal interfere with that plan. Albrecht will be furious when he hears about this and then we'll all suffer, not least your criminal.'

'If Albrecht sets foot in this house, then he will not leave alive,' said Henni, her quiet voice vibrating with menace.

'What? What the hell do you mean?'

'You know exactly what I mean, Magda.'

'You're mad, completely insane.'

Henni shrugged her shoulders. Loyalty to his wife stopped any further exchanges as Heinz insisted they leave. 'We have a long journey ahead of us.'

Magda turned to the nanny. 'Get in the truck.'

'No. Wanda stays here.'

'Heinz, for God's sake, tell her. I can't manage seven children without a nanny.'

His wife's narrowed eyes and compressed lips appalled him.

'I think you'll have to. Come on, let's get going. We'll discuss other options on the way.' And with that, he took Magda by the elbow and escorted her out of the farmhouse.

CHAPTER 4

'HEINZ... HEINZ.' HE HEARD the voice from far off, but it was only when Gunter shook his arm that he woke up.

'Here, I've made you some coffee.'

Heinz took the steaming cup and sat up, stretching his neck.

'Bad night?'

'Not the best.' The chaos of the family reunion was still vivid in his mind.

Gunter pulled up a chair and sat down next to him, sipping his drink.

'It's funny how you can get used to anything. I tell myself I'm going to have a cup of coffee and immediately I can smell it in the air and taste it on my lips and when the reality of this acorn substitute hits the back of my throat, I still pretend it's a proper coffee. The mind is a wonderful thing. Until it goes wrong, of course.'

Heinz held his cup in a firm grasp.

'Tell me something, Gunther. Is Henni capable of cold-blooded murder?'

'Whoa. Where has this come from?'

'I was thinking about what she said to Magda about Albrecht coming back and not leaving the house alive.'

'Oh, come on, that was months ago. You could see she was overwrought and desperate for Magda and the children to leave. She couldn't imagine having to provide food for that number of people and said whatever she needed to. She's always loved Albrecht. Why would she want to kill him?'

'I don't know.'

'Have you asked her?'

'No. I can't remember the last time we talked, really talked. I'm not even sure I know my wife anymore.'

'You must talk, or you will never understand. I can't tell you.'

'Tell me what?'

Gunter hesitated. 'How hard it has been for her here.'

'I realise it's all fallen on her shoulders, but we always used to be a team and now I feel she's cast me out with the rubbish.'

'Talk. That's all I can say. Now, I'd better feed the dogs and get them chained up for the day.'

Heinz took a mouthful of coffee. It was all very well for Gunter to tell him to talk, but hadn't he tried on numerous occasions? She was the one shutting him out, not the other way around. His eyes watered and he pressed a fist to his lips before dragging himself upstairs to get dressed.

The days passed. Heinz continued digging over the new vegetable plot, always keeping his senses alive to the possibility of Alp's return, checking for signals. Whenever he glanced up, Wanda was nearby. Since the episode with the spade, he avoided eye contact and was scrupulously polite. The more he ignored her, the more she played on his mind. He heard the swish of her dress, the clearing of her throat, the contented sigh. He glimpsed delicate fingers, muscled arms, long legs tucked into gardening boots. The south-facing plot grew warmer each day and he imagined it abundant with growth and the two of them celebrating their gardening success.

His dreams developed a sensual quality. He couldn't always remember what they entailed but a satisfied smile accompanied his catlike stretches before he leapt out of bed, eager to start the day. One morning he awoke surprised to find Henni still beside him. She always came to bed after he'd fallen asleep and was up preparing breakfast before he stirred. He leaned across and tentatively caressed her breast; she leapt out of bed as if he'd stung her with an electric prod.

'Henni, my sweet wife, what is this? It's as if you find me repulsive. Are we never going to make love again?'

'Repulsive? No, of course, not. Don't be silly. Look, I've got to get going. I can hear the children getting up. We'll talk another time, I promise.'

Heinz cursed under his breath and turned his head away. No sound came from the other bedrooms.

Mid-morning, she brought him a cup of coffee. He looked past her.

'Leave it on the bench, please. I'll drink it later.'

'I'm worried about Monika.'

Instantly, his resentment drained away.

'Why? What's happened?'

'Partly, I guess, she's growing up, but I sense there's

more to it than that. Do you remember when we moved to the farm when I was still pregnant with Lisle?'

Heinz nodded; it had been a painful few months for both of them.

'I noticed a real difference in her almost straight away. She relaxed and stopped obsessing about Hitler. She started reading all my childhood books – as you know, she's always loved reading – and they were just normal stories with none of the propaganda about Jews or anything else.

'I was so pleased. I thought she'd turned a corner, maybe even realised there was more to life than that evil bastard. But no, it wasn't to be. When your transfer to Krakow came through and we came to join you there, it all started up again. She started pestering me to join the Young Girls' League and then you remember how she carried on about getting another portrait of Hitler for the apartment and we started having to say Heil Hitler at the breakfast table again.'

'Don't remind me. How I hated that intrusion into our family life.'

'It's as if being here was like a holiday for her, a temporary lapse from her commitment to Nazism.'

'But you weren't in Krakow long, a few months at most. What happened when you returned here?'

'It was around that time that Mama started showing signs of dementia. Her behaviour became erratic, bizarre. She would say the strangest things and then be completely normal the next minute. She became my priority at least until the doctor gave us a diagnosis and we knew what to expect. I didn't neglect the children exactly, but I didn't spend as much time with them as I normally would. Perhaps she resented that. Oh, I don't know. The others have never been a worry. Tomas follows his grandfather around like a shadow and is in seventh heaven, being on the farm. Carola always seems contented with life no matter what and is surprisingly helpful in looking after Oma. It's just Monica who walks around with a permanent scowl on her face.'

'I haven't noticed the scowl, but she doesn't seem like her old, bubbly, and bossy self. Perhaps she misses her friends and school more than we realise. Do you want me to talk to her?'

'You can try, by all means. I'm not sure you'll get very far.'

'Well, I'll give it a go.'

'Thanks, Heinz. It's been good to talk about it.'

Heinz raised an eyebrow; the gesture was wasted on Henni who stood lost in her thoughts before turning back to the farmhouse.

A chance to win his wife over by solving the problem of their daughter. He turned his face to the sky and let the rays warm his face. When he picked up his spade again, he was humming Lili Marlene. He stopped just before lunch and surveyed his work. The plot was beginning to look good; he'd talk to Gunter about fertilizing it with cow manure before re-digging it with a fork. Or maybe it just needed a good raking over. He still knew little about gardening, let alone farming, but it surprised him how much he enjoyed this kind of work.

He'd loved his career as a police detective, and he knew he was good at it. His gut feel told him when people were lying, when things didn't feel right, when to apply pressure and when to back off. How he'd loved pitting his wits against the criminal mind. It wasn't always as dramatic as that; some criminals were just trapped in poverty and desperate for a way out; others were stupid and easily led. It was the psychopaths who needed to be removed from society as quickly as possible who fascinated him. He remembered one case with particular professional satisfaction: a serial killer who targeted prostitutes around Berlin. It wasn't his case, but the publicity was embarrassing the politicians as well as the police and they called him in to lend a hand.

He recalled the time wasters who always surfaced in these big cases: all manner of people confessing to the crime for God knows what psychological reasons. They even had a medium, a swarthy, gipsy grandmother, offering to solve the case for them. Instead, it was diligent police work that caught their killer and a measure of luck. A young woman walking home from her secretarial job had caught her heel in a drain cover; as she twisted her foot free, a man appeared from the shadows and offered to help her. Although he was polite and well-dressed, something about the encounter chilled her blood and she had the good sense to report the incident to the police. As he listened to her account, his guts told him it was significant. Her description of his accent as Northern, probably from Hamburg, was the clue he'd been waiting for.

Back in his office, he'd plotted the attacks and times on a wall map of Berlin. All were within easy walking distance of the main railway station. He checked the times of trains to and from Hamburg and laid his trap. Nothing happened for a couple of weeks; the overtime was ruinous, and his boss was losing patience. Then, on a Wednesday night, the killer struck. He mistook Bauer's decoy, a judo black belt no less, for a prostitute and attacked her. Instead, she floored him. Momentarily winded, he staggered away and then ran for his life.

Two detectives sitting in a nearby car were too slow off the mark, and he gave his pursuers the slip. Police soon discovered the felt hat he'd ditched en route to the station, and everyone felt confident of an imminent arrest. Bauer bided his time. He felt sure his serial killer was somewhere nearby, probably calmly drinking a beer in the station bar. He knew the next train to Hamburg was due in at 9pm; he also reasoned the killer would expect some police activity, so he had his uniformed colleagues wander around the station, checking random passengers before moving on. Nothing too aggressive, nothing to spook his target.

Bauer himself waited on the appropriate platform and watched as the passengers made their way onto the train. A family group passed him: the woman looked harassed as she held her daughter by the hand; her husband was giving their son a piggyback while clutching a large holdall. He strode ahead, the little boy giggling with pleasure, as the man bounced him about.

Bauer turned away and just as suddenly turned back. Something was wrong. He couldn't put his finger on it, but they just didn't seem like a proper family. He ran and boarded the train and found the woman settling into a compartment.

'Your husband? Where is he?'

'Back home in Hamburg.'

'But the man with you?'

'I don't know him. He just offered to help me aboard.'

'Of course. Thank you, Madam.'

It had to be him. He moved along the corridor, knowing he would recognise the man. And there he was, on his own in a compartment, staring out of the window.

'May I join you?'

The man shrugged just as a whistle blew and the train moved off. Bauer closed the door and removed his pistol from its holster. He pointed it at the passenger.

'If you move a single muscle, I won't hesitate to shoot you dead.'

The serial killer turned languidly and faced Bauer, hooded eyes locking into his, a sly grin creeping across his face.

'You didn't shoot me then?'

'Cocky, aren't you?'

'Why not? It took you long enough to find me. Nice touch with the judo bitch, by the way. Is she one of yours?'

'Social worker. She trained in judo to protect herself against some of the more unsavoury characters she has to deal with. Abusive husbands, that kind of thing. Black belt apparently.'

'I can believe it.'

'Do you want to tell me why you did it?'

'Not particularly. Kept me amused for a while.

A short while, sadly. Do you know how boring life is? Anything for a bit of excitement. Then the killing got boring. That surprised me, to be honest. Perhaps I should have targeted someone else? Social workers, maybe? The prostitutes became too easy but the stink of them lodged in my brain and I kept thinking if I kill another one then maybe the smell will go away. You deal with them, don't you, so you must be familiar with that cloying smell. Cheap perfume. Sweat. Previous customers. Hope.'

'Hope? Hope has a smell?'

He rolled his eyes. 'Obviously.'

'And what does hope smell of?'

He thought for a moment. 'Elderflowers, sometimes ashes. It depends on the circumstances.'

Fascinated, Bauer looked forward to continuing the conversation back at the police station. His prisoner yawned. Yellow teeth in a mottled grey-pink cavern.

'No, I've done everything I wanted to do in this life. I shall enjoy the trial. There will be a trial, won't there? Bit of drama to see me out and then whoosh as the guillotine drops. An adventure to end all adventures.'

There was a knock on the door. Bauer kept his gun trained on the prisoner.

'Enter.'

Two police colleagues slid the door open and waited.

'Handcuff him. One on each side of him. I don't want this one getting away.'

And that had been it. A serial killer arrested and public confidence in the police restored. The case had enhanced his reputation, but they had denied him the chance to interrogate the man and find out more about his olfactory intuition. He smiled. Happy times, times to be proud of, unlike the last few years. His work had become a chore, not least because he hated the regime that imposed his daily routine.

The pressure to join the Gestapo and the Nazi Party had been intense. Doing anything that went against the flow of enthusiasm for Hitler in those early days would have marked him out as suspect. He didn't need that when he had a young family to support. He never forgot the day a colleague repeated a joke about Hitler. It was some silly remark he'd overheard in the street. Minutes later he was marched out of the building and his desk cleared. He heard someone mutter "For a joke? Mein Gott" and then his boss called him into the office. Did he think Bauer had been the one to mutter? His stomach cramped.

'The Gestapo are looking for a man of your experience. You would be honoured, I think.'

'Yes, Sir.'

'Good. Don't spend too long thinking about it. It's not, shall we say, a matter for levity.'

Bauer flinched. Back at his desk, he rang his onetime mentor, retired Chief of Police, Ernst von Linden, and asked for a meeting that same evening. He tried to keep his tone light, but his voice squeaked like a trapped rodent. Their wide-ranging talk put things into perspective for Bauer and the sentiment his mentor expressed, that Bauer could do good wherever he served, clinched it for him. The next day he joined the Gestapo.

His work varied from investigating cases of disloyalty to the regime by fellow Germans to seeking out communist cells and, latterly, the resistance organisation in Krakow. Throughout he tried to stay faithful to the ideal of doing good. The more he witnessed brutality and relentless persecution, the more he tried to save lives. He had to avoid arousing suspicion so there was a limit to what he could achieve, as he was the first to admit. Still, there were hundreds of cases that owed their favourable outcome to him: sceptics given a stern warning instead of a prison sentence; houses searched in a cursory manner even though Bauer sensed the presence of conspirators; subtle warnings given to informers about forthcoming raids.

His bosses never questioned his techniques; as long as he brought in enough suspects for questioning and filed enough reports as closed, they judged him a loyal and productive member of the Party. Would it have made any difference if he had stayed in the Kriminalpolizei, the Kripo, instead of joining the Gestapo? Truthfully? He didn't think so. The process of Co-ordination or Gleichschaltung, as the Nazis called it, covered every area of life from education to the media to culture and the economy. Everything you said or did became the Nazi way of saying or doing. There was simply no escaping it unless you had a taste for martyrdom.

CHAPTER 5

Monika became the object of his attention over the next few days. She seemed to change from a playful little girl to a moody young lady and back again over a single morning. It was her relationship with her mother that worried Heinz the most. Whatever Henni said to her seemed to provoke that scowl. She was never disobedient, but she seemed to nurse some huge resentment against her mother.

He tested the waters himself, waiting until she was alone, away from the other children.

'Would you like to stay up a bit later tonight and play a game of cards with us?'

Her face lit up, and then the scowl appeared. 'Who with?'

'Me, your mother, Opa maybe, depending on whether Oma is calm enough to be left to her own devices.'

'What's wrong with Oma?'

He was certain they had discussed this before, but he let her change the subject.

'It's a disease of old age. Just as Opa has physical aches and pains in his joints and in his back from working hard all these years, so Oma has disturbances in her head which make her forget things and say strange things and do strange things.'

'Will she never get better?'

'No, I'm afraid not. All we can do is enjoy the times when she is lucid and able to be present with us and be patient with her when she doesn't understand what's going on.'

'I still love her, though.'

'Of course, you do. We all do. So, what about that game of cards?'

He could tell she was torn; he imagined that she desperately wanted to stay up late, so what was holding her back? Was it the prospect of playing cards with her mother? That seemed a little extreme.

'I guess that would be nice. Thanks, Papa, I'd like that.'

In the end, it was Wanda who made up a foursome together with Gunter. Henni pleaded a headache and said she would settle Lottie in bed before making an early night of it. Wanda partnered Monika as they played canasta against the men. It was a competitive evening, each side determined to win. At first, the cards favoured the girls; then their fortunes changed, and the men gained the upper hand. In the final nerve-racking round, the pile grew and grew until Monika picked it up with a triumphant yelp.

'Brilliant, Monika, well done,' said her partner, while the men groaned as she made canasta after canasta. The men commiserated with each other and decided to have a small Schnapps while Wanda offered to make a milk and honey drink for the two victors before they went to bed.

'That was fun,' said Monika. 'Can we do it again?'

'Yes, indeed. And don't imagine you'll win next time. Gunter and I will have a strategy meeting and decide how best we can beat you.'

Monika beamed at the challenge.

'Tell me, Gunter,' said Heinz once they were sitting alone enjoying a second drink. 'How do you find Monika?'

'What do you mean?'

'She's always been a very bright little girl, rather bossy to tell you the truth, but good-hearted and fond of her siblings. Now, it's as if she's going through some inner turbulence. Not all the time, of course, but often enough to be worrying. I wondered if it was anything to do with Hitler's death. She was a keen little Nazi, always keeping us on our toes with her Heil Hitlers and the propaganda she picked up at school.'

'Yes, Henni mentioned it once, but I must say I wasn't conscious of it. We were so far removed from all that nonsense here. Of course, we weren't stupid, and we kept a Nazi flag flying at the gateway to our farm to avoid any criticism. We had the occasional visit from Party officials, tedious men with nothing better to do than lecture us. Lottie and I used to become bobblehead dolls for the duration, nodding enthusiastically at everything they said. Thank God, her mind was sound then.

'When it got too much to bear, I used to say I had to tend the cows to provide food for the glorious Third Reich, and Lottie used to cut generous slices of cheese for them to take away. I worried it would encourage them to come back, but it's such a long way to climb up to the farm and I keep the farm gate locked against unwanted traffic, so it didn't happen that often. It helped that we're surrounded by farms, so they had plenty of places to choose from when they wanted food. It also helped that Albrecht was so high up in the SS and we weren't averse to mentioning our son-in-law, Inspector Bauer of the Gestapo.'

Heinz grinned. 'Yes, quite a killer combination. But tell me, lots of small farmers voted for the Nazis, why were you different?'

'I lost three sons in the Great War, as you know. That fact alone gave me a permanent dislike and distrust of anything political. Dieter and Wolfgang both died right at the beginning of the war in 1914 and Tomas died in 1916. It hit Lottie hard; in fact, I sometimes wonder if the repeated shocks were responsible for her current dementia. If physical problems can come back to haunt you in later life, then why not mental ones? Well, whatever, who can tell? Anyway, life was never the same for me after that. Everything I'd worked for all my life was to create a future for my children. To be honest, for my boys.

'It's not that I loved Henni any the less, far from it, but I always assumed she would get married and have her future taken care of by her husband. It was quite a worry when she remained single for so long. Too fussy by half, especially with the loss of menfolk, but she wouldn't compromise. "I'd sooner be an old maid than settle for someone I don't love and can't respect." That's what she told us whenever we raised the subject.

'Those first two years of war shattered all my dreams of working alongside my sons and leaving them the farm. Of course, there was always Albrecht.' Gunter stopped for a moment and looked shamefaced. 'I can't decide if it was me or Albrecht, but we never connected with each other the way I did with the others. As he grew older, he helped on the farm. He was a diligent worker when he put his mind to it, but his heart wasn't in it. When he joined the Party, he put all his enthusiasm into it, and it became harder and harder to get him to do any chores.

'It didn't help that he acted as if the sun shone out of Hitler's backside. God, he could be just as tedious as those Party officials. You must remember how he was when you visited with Henni after your marriage. I was embarrassed to be in the same room sometimes. Later, when I listened to Hitler's speeches on the radio, I tried to see him as Albrecht did, but all I could visualise was a giant toddler having a tantrum.

'Once he left for the General Government, we hardly ever heard from him. There would be the occasional postscript to Magda's letters, but she was the one who informed us about the births of our grandchildren. By the way, I meant to ask you, wasn't there an eighth baby?'

'Yes, he or she – I don't remember which – died after a premature birth.'

'Lottie was right, then, for all her dementia. It's sad that we've had nothing to do with them and probably won't in the future. After all, they're just as much our flesh and blood as your three are. Yet when they arrived, I felt nothing for them. I know they disappeared upstairs, and we all had other issues on our minds, but still, you'd expect us to be joyful or sad or disappointed or proud. Instead, we were just numb. Lottie was the same. There was no reaction from her afterwards, no upset, no questions, nothing. I find that a wretched situation. Mm, time for a top-up before I get maudlin.'

As Gunter poured their drinks, an owl hooted in the distance; its eerie call made Heinz think of Lisle lying cold in her grave. Had she known, in those few hours of life, that she was loved and wanted? He shook the image from his head.

'It always surprised me, when I first arrived back at the farm after dropping Magda off, how keen you were to set up the den and create a hiding place inside the house. I assumed I would be safe because the farm was so isolated, but you felt differently. Why?'

'Ask yourself this: what's the most dangerous animal in Germany? Think about it while I go for a pee.'

Heinz considered wild boar and then wondered about wolves or bears before rejecting them as zoo animals; Gunter came back inside, bolted the door, and interrupted his thoughts.

'So, have you worked it out? What's the most dangerous animal in Germany?'

Heinz shrugged.

'A cornered one.'

As soon as he said it, Heinz realised he was right.

'Because they have nothing to lose?'

'Exactly. Once the relentless bombing of our towns and cities started, the Nazis knew the end was coming, or at least most of them did. Of course, the sensible thing would have been to surrender, admit defeat, and stop the senseless killing of more innocent lives. But they couldn't do that for whatever reason: orders from above; Hitler's hypnotic influence on them; the memory of Versailles; fear of the consequences for them as individuals. So, they felt trapped and were determined to bring as many of us into the cage with them as possible.

'Anybody who had shown the slightest hesitation about adoring Hitler, whether at the beginning of his reign or towards the end, was earmarked for retribution. Bad enough that history was going to condemn those fanatics, they weren't about to let their neighbours sneer at them and enjoy any sense of triumph at the downfall of Nazism. I've lost count of the number of rumours I've heard about executions and hangings and ferocious repression of anything hinting at rebellion.'

'They're not just rumours. I've seen it for myself.'

'Is that so? Well, I'm not surprised. That's why we kept the flag flying at the entrance for so long and Albrecht's photo on prominent display. We even found a magazine photograph of Hitler and put that in a frame. God knows I wasn't going to waste money on a portrait, but it definitely became more dangerous around here, not less, as the war was ending.

'That's why I felt it was important to set up a den and a hiding place for you. Your career in the Gestapo will make you a target for the Americans, but I don't fear them as much as I feared our Gauleiter and his men hunting for deserters. I may be wrong, but I reckon the Americans will give you a fair trial. Those fanatics would have strung you up from the nearest tree as soon as look at you.'

'You're a wise man.'

'I don't know about that, but you get a lot of time to think when you're milking cows.'

'And you'll be turning my son into another philosopher.'

'He's a grand little boy, that's for sure. You'll never guess what he said to me the other morning. "Papa's frightened of cows and that's why they don't like him milking them." Came out with it just like that.'

'Really? Well, he's absolutely right about that. They look great in the field with their enormous eyes and tender mooing, but close up they give me the willies. And they've got a hefty kick when they want to show you who's boss.'

Gunter grinned. 'I'll tell you one thing. It's good to have another man around the farm, not just for the help you give me, but for the company. It's been a lonely few years. Then, when Lottie started to have her odd moments, I began to despair. I was very grateful when you let Henni return to the farm.'

'I'm not sure I could have stopped her.'

'Oh, you're wrong about that. She's always been a loyal wife and mother as far as I can see.'

'She never settled in Krakow, though. I hoped being able to see Albrecht and Magda on a regular basis would make it easier for her, but she visited them once with the children and then seemed reluctant to go again. I don't think they had a row or anything like that, but she wasn't keen on developing the relationship for whatever reason. Did she ever talk to you about it?'

'She did, a bit.'

'And?'

'She said Albrecht had changed beyond all recognition, that she didn't know him at all.'

'Humph. That sounds familiar.'

'Still not had your talk?'

'No, not yet.'

'Well, time for bed. Those cows won't milk themselves in the morning. Goodnight Heinz.'

'Goodnight Gunter. I'll follow you up shortly.'

Was it his imagination or had Gunter cut short their conversation to avoid talking about Henni's assessment of her little brother? He had been adamant that Henni loved Albrecht and that her threat to kill him had been words pulled out of the air to get rid of Magda, but he wasn't so sure. Her tone of voice, her steely determination, suggested pre-planning rather than random threats. He wished he could recall what she'd said at the time in Krakow; she definitely said that Albrecht didn't understand how difficult farming had become for her elderly parents and then she pressed her husband to take early retirement to help them.

That just hadn't proved possible. His boss had been typically unsympathetic. Everyone had to make sacrifices and if farming was that onerous for his parents-in-law they could always apply for some slave labour. Heinz supposed they couldn't have kept him working against his will; he could have resigned, but then they could have decided they needed another volunteer for the Eastern front. He wondered if his request for early retirement had got back to Albrecht.

What had happened to Albrecht? The Russians entered Krakow on the 19th of January, long after Albrecht had been due to join his family in Bavaria. Had he missed his opportunity to get away? Had he changed his mind, or had it changed for him? And why hadn't he come after Heinz as he had threatened to do? And yet, all the passes he had provided were one way only. Was it a message for Heinz to stay away? To avoid returning to Krakow at all costs?

Heinz longed for clarity. He wanted to believe he had done the right thing and that he had nothing to fear from Albrecht, whether directly or through someone like Alp. Surely Alp could find out what had become of Albrecht. Even if he didn't know him, Albrecht was high enough up the chain of command for his fate to be known. Heinz looked at his empty glass. He fancied another but didn't like to help himself in Gunter's home. There was nothing for it but to go to bed.

He went upstairs taking care to avoid the steps that creaked. He heard Gunter talking quietly to Lottie and her chuckled reply. She was having a lucid moment. He chewed at his lips; this was what marriage should be like. When he entered their bedroom, Henni was fast asleep; at one time, her gentle snores would have soothed him, but tonight he was far too wound up to sleep. He stared out of the window and listened to the sounds of the night: the occasional yip of the farm dogs running free; an anguished screech from a hunted creature; the hoot of an owl; swaying branches creaking and groaning in the distance.

Was it really only six months since he'd driven away from the farm with a furious Magda sitting at his side? Her fury had been palpable that night: she had planted her boots astride, limbered up her shoulders and neck like a prize fighter, clenched and unclenched her hands.

'She won't get away with this, the evil bitch.' Spittle hit the windscreen. 'I told Albrecht to arm me. This would look very different if I owned a gun. The stupid, stupid cow.'

Heinz winced and gripped the steering wheel hard. He loved his wife and even though the reunion had been far from satisfactory, the sight of Henni had stirred up his emotions. He belonged at her side, not travelling through the night like this. He needed to find a way of being with her before this tedious war ended.

'I know she's your wife and I'm sure you're very loyal to her and all that, but there is more at stake here than what she wants or what she gets to decide. When did she become Lord Almighty of all she surveys? And, what the hell did she mean when she said she'd kill Albrecht if he ever stepped foot inside the farm?'

Heinz wondered that himself but thought it best not to inflame the situation by commenting. She unbraided her hair and ran her hands through it until she resembled a Gorgon.

'You said Albrecht had planned this for all of us. What was the plan?'

'The war's over, Heinz. The Jews have done for us. We'll never win now. With their money supporting the Bolshevik hordes, we'll be lucky to escape with our lives.'

'What Jews? We've been rounding them up into ghettos and camps since 1939 and making them pay for the privilege. I doubt there are many Jews left on the outside now and even less of their money.'

'More fool you.' She jabbed a finger at him, nostrils flaring. 'Don't you understand anything? They're like vermin who breed faster than you can kill them. Trust me, their networks cover the entire world from Britain to America to Switzerland to Everywhere.'

She made the word "everywhere" sound like a war cry.

'They've been plotting and scheming and infiltrating our enemies. They're devious bastards. Always have been. God only knows what they've been up to and what damage they've caused to our beloved Fuehrer. They caused our downfall at Versailles and they haven't stopped since.'

'I don't think I've got the energy for this. Anyway, you haven't told me what the plan was.'

'Albrecht didn't give me all the details. He just said it would be best for us to stick together as a family and make use of the farm's isolation. He would join us as soon as Hitler gave the command.'

'To surrender?'

'No, of course not. To regroup, ready to fight again. That's how Albrecht put it. Like a tactical retreat although he never used the word retreat because it maddened Hitler whenever anyone suggested retreating.'

'But if you're right and the war is over, then why regroup to fight again? It doesn't make sense.'

'It does if you love the Fuehrer. This war is over but another, greater one is only just beginning.'

'Magda, aren't you tired of all this? Wouldn't you like to settle down and bring up your children in peace?'

'There can be no peace while the Fuehrer's enemies are still alive.'

Heinz sighed and focused on the road ahead. Magda continued to twitch in her seat, muttering threats under her breath as if Henni rode alongside them. The windscreen fogged up, and Heinz opened his window. Cold evening air filled the cab; a clean scent like freshly ironed linen tinged with pine teased his nostrils and calmed his senses.

He didn't know what to make of it all. His wife had always been strong, but he'd never detected any violence in her. She wasn't even quick to anger. She'd meant every word, though; he was certain of that. The greater problem was working out what to do with Magda, the smouldering volcano threatening to erupt.

'Tell me about your family. How do you think they will react when they see you?'

'My mother will be delighted to meet her grandchildren. It's the only saving grace to this change of plan.'

'Has she never seen any of them?'

'Only the first two.'

'That's a shame.'

'It couldn't be helped. My place was with my husband, and Albrecht was posted to Krakow within days of the invasion. He works so hard for the Fuehrer. He never stops and his responsibilities are vast, unbelievably vast. I needed to make sure his life was carefree when he arrived home at night. There was no way I could take off for visits to my parents just to satisfy their desire to see their grandchildren.'

'Did they pressure you to visit?'

'They did, at first. Then I wrote to them and told them to stop pestering me or they'd never see their grandchildren again.'

'I see. Wasn't that a bit harsh?'

'No. Sometimes you have to be cruel to be kind. In fact, I'm beginning to think you always have to be cruel to be kind. People overreact to little things because they fail to see the bigger picture. You must be firm with people to get them to see sense. It wouldn't do you any harm to take that approach with Henni. You and Gunter, for that matter. If you'd both put your feet down, we wouldn't be back in this bloody truck.'

A thin wail pierced the air.

'I think we should stop and check on the children.'

'They'll be fine.'

'All the same, I need to stretch my legs.'

'Oh, very well, if you insist.'

Heinz parked up and left the engine running. He walked round to the rear of the truck, thinking how heartless Magda was. Henni would never have let her children suffer.

'Are you all right?'

'Peter is crying.'

'Do you know why?'

'His nappy needs changing.'

'Yes, he smells.'

A chorus of 'pooh' did nothing to calm the angry little boy.

'Where is Wanda?' The eldest girl's tone was as

belligerent as her mother's. Heinz walked round to Magda's side of the cab.

'The little one needs his nappy changing.'

'Well, since you think I can do without Wanda, I suggest you do it. You'll find clean nappies and a damp flannel in the navy bag.'

How difficult could it be? Henni had changed plenty of nappies in front of him. He didn't feel like arguing with Magda and he couldn't leave Peter crying his eyes out. He thought through the process, retrieved the newspaper he'd been saving to read, and returned to the rear of the truck.

'Right children, pass Peter across to me and find me the navy bag.'

He laid a now furious toddler onto the newspaper, took off his trousers and dirty nappy, and, reeling somewhat from the stench, wiped his bottom with a cold, damp flannel. Murdering the poor child would have elicited fewer screams. He used a clean nappy to dry him and then folded him into a fresh one and back into his trousers.

'There, little one, that wasn't so bad, was it?' Peter didn't agree and continued crying.

'Now, children, do any of you want to get out for a wee?'

One by one, they clambered over the edge of the truck and ran to the nearest bushes. By the time they'd all made it back inside, Peter's crying had subsided into half-hearted sobs and hiccups. Heinz handed the boy over to the eldest girl and instructed them all to settle down to sleep. It would be a frosty night, but they had plenty of blankets and could make themselves cosy.

He tucked the navy bag along one side and pondered what to do with the dirty nappy. Clothing of any description had become scarce in the last years of the war and no doubt nappies were hard to find too; still, he didn't have another bag and didn't want the stench in the cab or in the back with the children. In the end, he placed the nappy on the newspaper and left them on the side of the road.

'You're full of surprises. I don't think Albrecht would be able to change a nappy if you put a gun to his head.'

'Needs must.'

'I'm getting cold; can you shut that window now?'

CHAPTER 6

THE TRUCK RUMBLED THROUGH the night. He missed a turning and had to double back. Fatigue caused his eyelids to droop; he clenched the steering wheel hard and tried to shake himself awake.

'It's no good. I'm going to have to take a break and get some sleep or we'll end up crashing.'

A thin column of light shone through the trees ahead and he turned into a roadside farmstead where a curtain was askew. When he knocked with his fist, the light went out and some kind of heavy object hit the door with undisguised violence. His heartbeat raced. Had he just endangered the lives of seven small children?'

'What do you want?' A barrel-chested man clutching a sawn-off shotgun limped towards him from the side of the farmhouse. He wheezed and had difficulty catching his breath. There was another thump at the door. Jittery fingers played with the gun.

'That's my brother.' He coughed, scrutinising Bauer. 'He doesn't take kindly to being disturbed.'

'I apologise for the inconvenience. I'm Heinz Bauer of the Gestapo escorting this family to the village of Gerstenried. Perhaps you know it?'

'No.' The tone remained truculent, and Bauer decided to change tack.

'Did you know the light from your farmhouse was visible from the road?'

'Can't be doing more harm than the headlights from your truck.'

'Except my truck is on the move, unlike your window.'

'Not now it isn't.'

Bauer snorted and relaxed. Alarmed by the show of violence and now wide awake, he had planned to get back in the truck and keep driving; instead, he found himself liking the man's spirit and judged they would be safe here. His decision was punctuated by another thump at the door.

'Tell your *brother*, or maybe just your wife, that we mean no harm. We just need somewhere to stay the night, and then we'll be on our way. And we'll pay for any inconvenience caused.'

'Pay? How much?'

Bauer suggested a figure. The old man doubled it and they argued about it until he settled for a sum halfway in between.

Honour satisfied, the farmer shifted his weight from foot to foot and lowered his gun.

'How many are you?'

'A mother with her seven children and me.'

'It'll be a tight squeeze.'

'We don't mind that and thank you...'

'Wolfgang.'

'Thank you, Wolfgang.'

A short while later seven wide-eyed children sat in front of an open fire, sipping warm milk from a variety of cups and mugs. Wolfgang's wife, Elisabeth, fussed around them, breaking into a toothless grin at regular intervals. As Heinz had suspected, Wolfgang didn't have a brother. The gentle babble of childish voices mingled with the roar and crackle of burning logs; unpredictable sparks rushed up the chimney and occasionally into the room making the children shriek with excited laughter.

Wolfgang and Heinz were making inroads into the roughest hooch he'd ever swallowed and sharing a platter of smoked sausages and cheese. He took in his surroundings and frowned. There was something peculiar here. A fireplace and a range seemed rather extravagant in the same room, even with its large dimensions. Some of the furniture was rough-hewn; other pieces were select and refined. He was no connoisseur, but the landscape paintings on the walls exuded a quality of light and texture that put him in mind of some of the great masters, even if he couldn't name them off the top of his head. No reason why they couldn't have copies, of course, but it jarred, nonetheless.

'Tell me, Wolfgang, have you and Elisabeth lived here long?'

'Long enough.' He blinked and looked towards the door.

'Anyway, what have they done?' He jerked his head towards Magda and the children.

'Nothing. I'm escorting them home as a favour to Magda's husband.'

'He must be important to take you away from your other work.'

'He is. Your paintings are rather special. Tell me about them.'

'There's nothing to tell. Waste of money if you ask me.'

Wolfgang kept his eyes averted and knocked back his drink, causing a fit of coughing and spluttering. When the commotion was over, he replenished both glasses and ordered Elisabeth to bring them some beers.

'This stuff needs a chaser, or your head will pound like a drum tomorrow.'

Heinz waited for the beers and resumed the conversation.

'So why buy them?'

'What?'

'The waste of money paintings.'

Wolfgang's jowly face tightened in front of him.

'Now, look here. You can quit your bloody interrogation. We've done nothing wrong, and we didn't have to let you into our home and give you our hospitality whether you're paying for it or not. She likes the paintings, so they stay; otherwise, I'd put them on the fire and be done with them.'

The angry outburst caused him to wheeze again. Heinz leant back in his chair, amused by the guilty conscience turning ears red and features contorted.

'Relax, Wolfgang. I'm not here on official business. I'm just interested.'

'Pah.'

In an amiable, conversational tone Heinz continued: 'Take the rocking chair you're sitting in.

Solid, comfortable, goes back generations I shouldn't wonder.'

'That it does. Belonged to my great-grandfather. I can still remember him rocking in it when I was a small boy. He lived to a grand old age; not something I'm likely to do with these lungs.'

'You're good for another fifty years, at least. You came round the farmhouse fast enough with your gun at the ready.'

He looked mollified at the compliment.

'That's the sort of furniture I like. Robust, suited to its purpose. Now take that cabinet over there. Very fine craftsmanship, I grant you, but useless in a farmhouse. Put a bit of weight on it and it would collapse.'

'Ha, yes, nearly did when I had a coughing fit and leant on it.'

'There you go. That's exactly what I mean.'

Heinz picked another slice of sausage, closed his eyes, and smelled the peppery warmth and garlic.

'These are damned good sausages. Do you make them yourselves?'

'That we do.'

'So, what's the story?'

Wolfgang took a swig of beer and sucked his lips. 'You don't give up easily, do you?'

'Years of training but I meant what I said: I'm not here on official business and your story will go no further unless, of course, you've committed a crime.'

'Like I said, we've done nothing wrong. They asked us to take care of it. Came all the way to our farm to do it. They were almost humble about it which wasn't like them at all.'

'Who?'

'The Yids.'

'Ah.'

'Told us they were leaving and wouldn't be back for a while. Could we keep an eye on the place, and could we send them the small parcel they brought with them as soon as they sent us a forwarding address? Gave us some money for the postage costs.'

'What was in it?'

'What makes you think I looked?'

'Call it my experience of human nature.'

'I didn't look immediately I'll have you know. But as the weeks turned into months and we got no word from them, I opened it up. There were gold coins, a ring, some other jewellery, all wrapped up in newspaper.'

Wolfgang's eyes sparkled at the memory.

'So, when did you move in here?'

'About the same time, maybe a bit earlier. The land's better quality here and there's more of it. I used the gold to increase my stock and then I applied for workers to help us on the farm. Had two of them – a couple of Ukrainians, I think, or maybe Poles. Can't remember now. Some eastern European country anyway. They weren't farming stock, that's for sure.'

'What do you mean?'

'Didn't have a bloody clue. Had to show them how to do everything. Spent as much time doing that as farming. Used to tell Elisabeth I was better off on my own. After a couple of years, they got a bit better. Once they'd got a few callouses on their hands, they started to know what's what.

'I reckon we ought to be paid to take them on. Free board and lodging and I've taught them useful skills into the bargain. All they gave me was aggravation. Sullen faces, hard stares. I kept my shotgun with me at all times, I can tell you. There was no need for that attitude. We didn't treat them bad. Well, we didn't spoil them, of course. Your mates in the Gestapo made it clear we had to be firm with them or lose them to another farm.'

'Where are they now?'

'Long gone, ungrateful bastards. They buggered off not long after we got the harvest in. I suppose I should be grateful it didn't happen sooner. I told the local militia, and they hunted for them, but I didn't hold out much hope. They took enough food to keep them going for weeks. And they took my Luger. I kept it hidden in one of the cooking pots. That way Elisabeth could use it if there was any trouble. Guess they must have chanced upon it when they came looking for supplies.'

'What's happened to your own farm?'

'It's still there. I keep an eye on it. Use the fields for additional pasture. Check the farmhouse is watertight. If my son makes it back from the war, then he can have it. If he doesn't, then I'll sell it.'

'And what if the owners come back?'

'Do you think they will?'

'Could be.'

'Nah, I don't reckon so. Not from what I hear. Anyway, they chose to leave. Nobody forced them. By now I've got some rights too. Place would have collapsed without my work on it. Once a roof leaks, and this one did, it's only a question of time before the whole lot rots away and the vermin move in. If they do come back, they'll have a fight on their hands to get the place back.'

Heinz sagged in his chair and sipped his beer in despair. Where did this anti-Semitism come from? He couldn't understand it. He'd had Jewish friends at school; he owed his life to a Jew in the Great War; his parents had had Jewish friends. Admittedly, they had all worn their religion lightly and were as German as he was. But even when he came across Orthodox Jews wearing their black hats, long coats, and dangling sidelocks, he was simply interested in their beliefs and customs. It didn't arouse any hatred in him.

Wolfgang's Yids had been wealthier than him and had, he seemed to suggest, looked down on him. Perhaps envy and a desire to prove he was just as good as they were made him oblivious to their plight? Claiming they chose to leave and that nobody forced them... surely Wolfgang didn't really believe that?

Deep in thought, Heinz missed the children being put to bed and suddenly registered he was alone with Wolfgang, who was making inroads into another bottle of hooch. He waved it at him.

'No, thank you, but I'd happily join you in another beer.'

'Help yourself. They're in the kitchen, under the sink. Bring me one while you're about it.'

They sat in silence for a while; Bauer watched his host sneak glances at him and gathered the man wanted to talk.

'So, tell me about your son. Did you just have the one boy?'

'That we did. I could never make it out, to tell you the truth. You see, we had to get married; Elisabeth was pregnant, and her father threatened to batter me into a pulp if I didn't do right by her. Which I would have done without the threats. I thought she was a great girl. The pregnancy went well, and she gave birth to Wilhelm with no problem at all. We named him after her father to make things right with him, and he soon became a besotted grandfather. I was out in the fields when she went into labour and by the time I got home, the baby had already been born. Good healthy weight, fine tackle, if you know what I mean, and the loudest pair of lungs I've ever heard. And that was it.

'I got her pregnant several times after that. There was never a problem with that side of things, I can assure you, but something always went wrong, and she lost them. I was cut up about it, too, but it's a bitter pill for a woman to swallow. It's what they're there for, isn't it? Having babies. If they can't do that, well, what's the point?'

Bauer, who had rather more enlightened views about the role of women, considered responding, but ended up nodding sympathetically.

'You could see how delighted she was to have Magda's brood to look after tonight,' he said.

'You see, that's the other thing I don't understand. Wilhelm's nearly 40 now. He should have been married and fathering his own kids long ago. It would have made such a difference to Elisabeth if she could have been a grandmother, looking after her own flesh and blood.

'He was always popular with the girls. Good-looking lad, if I say so myself, but he never pursued things to the end. The girls got fed up waiting to be asked and married someone else. What's that all about, then? Why the hesitation? Why not just buckle down and get on with it? Marriage, children, it's the way of the world. No point resisting it.

'I tried talking to him about it and, give him his due, he always listened and seemed to accept the point I was making. But nothing ever happened. You're a man of the world, what do you think was the issue?'

Bauer took a sip of his beer. Homosexuality was his immediate gut feel, but he didn't suppose that answer would go down well with his host. Wolfgang probably didn't care too much about its illegality or the Nazi regime's determination to persecute its practitioners, but the man was keen to have grandchildren ostensibly for his wife's sake and most likely his own. He remembered his conversation with Gunther and his desire to leave the farm to his sons. Most parents wanted to leave something to their children whether it was property or possessions, but he suspected the instinct was even stronger among farmers. There was something intimate about the way they tended the land; they didn't just work hard; they invested their heart and soul in it. Seeing the land go to strangers would hurt like hell.

'Where is Wilhelm now?'

'Joined the army as soon as Hitler declared war. He wasn't one for writing, so I've no idea where he is now.'

'He's still young, though, I wouldn't worry about it

too much. War has a way of maturing young men and making them appreciate how important having a family is.'

'Let's hope you're right and that he doesn't come back a cripple or in a box.'

CHAPTER 7

TRYING TO SETTLE IN a pull-out bed placed next to the dying fire, Bauer wondered if his instinct about the young man's homosexuality was right. He pulled a wry face as he remembered investigating a Polish woman caught carrying a gun for the resistance. A spirited woman, she'd diverted their attention away from her own situation and onto a homosexual German officer. He'd never been convinced of the man's existence, but the hunt kept one of his more unpleasant colleagues occupied for weeks. They'd sent her to Ravensbrück concentration camp, he recalled, and wondered how she had fared there.

He slept fitfully, moving in and out of nightmare scenarios, convinced he had to get back home but unable to find his way in yellow-grey fog, in stinking trenches, in open fields with machine gun fire splattering his face with mud. Voices called to him from different directions urging him on but which path was the right one?

The next morning Bauer woke with a throbbing headache to find Magda staring at him, two cups of coffee in her hands.

'I wouldn't mind staying here.'

'Oh?' He sat up, groaned, and pressed his hands against his eyes before taking one of the coffees.

'Elisabeth is a damned sight more help at her advanced age than Wanda ever was. She's bathed all the children, fed them breakfast and now she's telling them all a story. They're engrossed in it.'

'I expect she misses having grandchildren of her own to fuss over. They only had the one son and he never married, according to Wolfgang.'

'What a shame. Perhaps I could leave them some of mine? Good grief, look at your face. It's all right, Heinz, I was only joking.'

'Of course. Look, give me a few minutes. I'll feel more sociable when I've had a wash and some breakfast.'

Back in the truck heading for Gerstenried, Magda seemed cheerful and talkative.

'Tell me something, Magda, back home you described Wanda as a criminal. What was her crime?'

'She's a Jehovah's Witness. Blind obedience to God at all times and subversive to the Third Reich as a result.'

Heinz swallowed the obvious response.

'I don't think I've ever met one. I don't know that much about them. I know they refused to do military service or give allegiance to the Fuehrer which, of course, made them enemies of the state, but they didn't come under my department; there was a distinct branch of the Gestapo which infiltrated their meetings and put a stop to their activities.'

He tried to remember what the nanny looked like. 'So, did it ever bother you having a criminal under your roof?'

'No, I knew I was safe. That's the thing with the Witnesses, they are so moral and so honest that they never even tried to escape from the camps or from the houses they worked in. You could leave all the doors unlocked and they wouldn't walk out. Completely bizarre in my opinion, but incredibly useful fodder for domestic servants.

'Albrecht told me you could beat them to a pulp and they still wouldn't say "Heil Hitler". I used to leave food out, but it didn't matter how hungry they were, they never stole any of it.'

'Was that honesty or fear of being beaten to a pulp?' He tasted bile as Magda laughed in response.

'Well, you'll be able to ask her next time you see her, won't you?'

'I guess so.' He didn't understand why Henni had insisted on keeping the nanny, but the thought was peripheral to his aim of being reunited with his wife and children. How to achieve the impossible played on his mind incessantly.

Magda rested her feet against the dashboard and gazed at her surroundings. 'I'm quite looking forward to getting home. I rather think my mother will be just like a younger version of Elisabeth, delighted to be surrounded by her grandchildren and keen to make the most of every minute.'

'I expect you're right. Lottie used to be like that before the dementia took hold.'

'Yes, I don't envy Gunter dealing with that. Or Henni for that matter.'

'That's kind of you. You seem to have forgiven Henni for her outburst, or am I mistaken?'

'Forgiven? What are you? A part-time priest? No,

I'm not interested in that wishy-washy stuff. It's more that I'm practical about life. If I could have changed the situation by being armed, for example, then I would have done so.

'What Henni said and the way she behaved was appalling, but I'm going to leave Albrecht to sort all that out when he rejoins us. It'll be interesting to see what he wants to do about it. I imagine he'll be furious at having his plans changed, but you'll have to deal with that in the first instance.'

Heinz shuddered at the prospect.

'He won't *forgive* Henni; still, that's her lookout. Of course, by the time he reaches us, he could well have different priorities. He's not one to waste energy on distractions. In any case, I suspect he makes too much of the farm's isolated position. Better to be in a village surrounded by true believers than out in the sticks surrounded by who knows what kind of people, probably the sort to put out a white flag as soon as they hear gunfire in the distance.

'Besides, the decision to leave was made so quickly by Albrecht that I didn't have time to work out all the details of cohabiting with Henni. I thought her devotion to her younger brother would smooth out any potential problems. But I had a long chat with Elisabeth last night and she warned me about the dangers of two women sharing one kitchen. I can see exactly what she meant. It's different if you're in your mother's house because everything you've learnt you've learnt from her. Put two different approaches to housekeeping in one kitchen and boom: it's a recipe for disaster.'

Magda rabbited on, requiring little to no input from Heinz who allowed his mind to wander avenues of escape. His was a growing conviction that returning to Krakow would be the biggest mistake of his life. Her analysis of Jewish involvement was wrong, but Magda was right about the war being over. Defeat didn't bother him; he just didn't want to die in a foolish last-ditch stand against the enemy, with people like Albrecht fighting alongside him. Heinz felt no kinship with him or his political views; no belief in a just cause or a Greater Germany or a beloved Fuehrer spurred him on. He wanted peace at any price. What was the phrase people were using all over Germany? An end with horror rather than a horror without end.

The question was: how could he achieve his own end with horror? He would have to deliver Magda to her parents and pretend to head back to Krakow. Then what? His best chance of survival would be back at the family farm, but it was also the first place Albrecht would send his henchmen to root him out. Would they shoot him on the spot? In front of his family? Or take him back for a show trial and hang him with a placard around his neck as a warning to other traitors?

Perhaps death in battle was preferable, after all? Either way, death beckoned. Death.

'Oh, my God.'

'What?'

He blurted the words out in astonishment: a solution had popped into his brain like a magic lantern slide.

'It's nothing. I just thought of something related to a

problem at work. A fresh approach which might solve a case I'm working on.'

That was it. That's what he had to do – stage his own death. The idea gave him hope and without realising it, he was speeding along the road. Magda whooped in delight. 'Wow, a secret speed freak! This is how Albrecht likes to drive, throwing caution to the winds.'

'Sorry, Magda, for a moment there I forgot I wasn't on my own.' He slowed to a sensible speed.

'Don't mind me. I love it. You can't beat that feeling of being as free as the wind, especially on the back of a motorbike.'

'I can imagine. This truck has some oomph, though, doesn't it? What a shame I need to consider the safety of our passengers in the back as well as yours.'

'Yes, I suppose. I'm surprised you don't want to stop and check they're all right.'

'Do you think we should?'

'No.'

Towards lunchtime, as they approached Magda's village, a motley selection of youngsters and old men moved from the ditches to block the road. Their black and red armbands proclaimed them as members of the Volkssturm, or Hitler's people's army. Dressed in civilian clothing, they sported a variety of headgear like a Sunday outing from a menswear shop.

Heinz slowed to a halt; their dour faces oozed resentment as they fiddled with their weapons: a few stout clubs, an old-fashioned rifle or two, and a single anti-tank Panzerfaust. Lollipops against the massed forces of the Allied advance. These were the men who would fight to the last breath in their bodies to save the Fatherland from destruction. God help them.

'I'll let them know why we're here.'

Heinz jumped out of the cab and strode towards them. He stopped, gave the Heil Hitler salute, and sauntered forward, holding out his Gestapo identification. This was examined by their leader, the only man wearing a military-style peaked cap. Minutes later, they strolled back to the truck.

'Magda, is that you?'

'Uncle Dieter! How wonderful to see you!' With genuine delight, Magda leapt from the cab and arm in arm with "her dearest uncle" escorted him to the rear of the truck to introduce her brood. Heinz stayed in sight of the army; he didn't want them getting nervous and firing off their missile.

Leaning against the truck, he gave his death careful thought. Geography had favoured him, and he could return most of the way to the farm before disposing of the truck and covering the last few miles on foot. By pure chance, he'd established himself as a speed enthusiast who would accept risks driving on his own. He would have preferred to die nearer Magda's home than his own; better for Albrecht to hear the news of his demise from her. Still, there was nothing he could do about that; he wouldn't be able to carry many provisions and the weather was turning bitter; he didn't want to die from hypothermia.

A salvo of gunfire startled him. The Volksstrum leader reappeared with Magda.

'What the hell was that?' said Heinz, fearing for the safety of his nieces and nephews.

'A firing squad, I would imagine.'

'That's not in your remit, surely? Are the Wehrmacht stationed here?'

'No, we don't need the army to solve our problems. What we've got is traitors: villagers who think we should betray our Fuehrer instead of fighting the enemies who would destroy us and destroy our way of life.'

'That's the spirit.' Magda applauded her uncle with a gleam in her eye and her chin held high. 'God, I wish I'd been born a man. I'd know exactly what to do with traitors.'

Heinz had a sinking feeling she still included Henni in that definition. He was desperate to leave.

'Are we clear to carry on?'

'Absolutely. See you later, Magda.'

'I look forward to it, Uncle.'

The gunfire had invigorated the Volksstrum soldiers who were marching back into the village and singing Horst-Wessel-Lied at the top of their voices as if their lives depended on it. Heinz checked the mirror as he passed them and pitied them. His mood changed as he drove into the little square marking the centre of Gerstenried.

A woman bowed down with grief, clutched a small child to her stomach, and wept. A few feet away the body of a man lay outstretched; congealed blood sat in a pool on his chest. Heart pounding, he counted two more bloody corpses. A body hanging from a bare-branched tree was being lowered to the ground. Another woman rushed over and flung herself at him, rocking his dead body in her arms, caressing his features with her hand, talking to him all the while. A second body was still hanging there.

'My home is just over there,' said Magda, pointing out a house on the corner of an adjacent street. Was she oblivious to the scene playing out in front of them? Did she not have a gram of pity? Not trusting himself to speak, Heinz manoeuvred the truck around the square and parked outside her house.

'Here we are then.'

Controlling every muscle in his body, Heinz turned his lips up in a tight smile and busied himself with helping the children out of the truck. Magda hoisted Peter onto her hip and clutching the second youngest by the hand, went up to the door and pushed it open. Heinz ushered the other children towards their mother as exclamations of surprise and delight filled the air. He called out that he needed to move the truck; nobody seemed to take any notice; he slammed the door shut and drove off at speed.

At the edge of the village, he parked up and kept slamming his hands into the steering wheel until they hurt more than his aching jaw. What a mess it all was: vigilantes had taken over the world and were murdering anyone who stood in their way or voiced a contrary opinion. But why was he surprised? They were only doing on a smaller scale what Hitler had sanctioned throughout Europe. The chief fanatic inspiring other fanatics. One thing was clear: he had to get back to his wife and family. More than ever, he needed to tread carefully and use any opportunities that came his way.

He drove back. Uncle Dieter was remonstrating with a group of villagers. The grieving women had disappeared. He parked the truck and came over to them, treading softly as he approached. He could make this work to his advantage.

'We're not leaving them here to rot. The sight upsets the women, and it's just not right.' The man who spoke was small and wizened.

'You're right, it isn't. It makes the place look a mess apart from anything else. And you can't argue that we need them as a deterrent. After today's activities, there isn't a soul who would dare say a word against Hitler.' His companion was a burly man who could have been a blacksmith in his youth, judging from his muscular arms and weather-beaten face.

'Well, who's going to do it? I've dismissed my men for the day,' said Dieter.

'Can't they do it tomorrow?' The whining voice came from an elderly man on crutches, one trouser leg folded in half.

'I'm not happy about it. They'll do what they're ordered, of course, but they're not gravediggers. They're soldiers defending the Fatherland. I don't want to piss them off with graveyard duties.'

'We should have made them dig their own pits before we shot them,' said the blacksmith type.

'Yeah, bit late now,' said Dieter. 'Could make the widows do it…'

'Have a heart. Besides, my wife would go mad. And I'm betting she wouldn't be the only one,' said the wizened villager.

'Gentlemen?' Suspicious faces turned to face him.

'Am I correct in thinking you have a problem with the disposal of these bodies?'

Dieter introduced Heinz to the others, who remained suspicious.

'May I suggest something? We passed the municipal dump on our way here. I'm returning that way later and I could easily tip the bodies out there.'

'Yes. Yes, definitely. Why not indeed?' Most of the others echoed Dieter's response.

'Hang on a minute. What do we tell the widows?'

'That we buried them in accordance with the law. That should shut them up. They're hardly likely to go looking for them at the dump. In any case, as chance would have it, Hans does his weekly delivery there tomorrow. We just need to warn him to keep shtum. By the time he's pitched his load on top of the corpses, there'll be nothing for anyone passing by to see.'

'I don't like it.'

'Why not?'

'It took three women to peel Ingrid off her husband. It would be kinder to let her have a body to bury.'

'Kinder?' The sneer in Dieter's voice silenced his wizened opponent. 'We're not the bleeding Red Cross. Fritz was a traitor, and he got what was coming to him. The sooner she takes that on board, the better for her and everyone else. Got it?'

'Yes, but...'

'But what?'

'Well, if they were buried in accordance with the law then there's going to be a grave somewhere.'

'Yes, and the law states that traitors are buried anonymously so that nobody can identify them and turn them into martyrs with shrines and flowers and all that nonsense.'

'Oh, right. I guess that makes sense.'

'So, are you happy now?'

'Yes.'

'Excellent. The plan's a good one. Bloody good, actually. Manfred, will you check the bodies for any identifying items – wallets, papers, that kind of thing? Be extra careful going through the stranger's pockets. We don't want that one coming back to haunt us.'

'Stranger?' asked Heinz.

'Yes, interfering git. Started protesting that we couldn't set up a firing squad without a court martial. You know the kind of thing. Thinks he's a bloody lawyer when he knows nothing about what's been going on here. I argued with him for a bit and then we strung him up alongside Fritz so he could watch from a vantage point.'

Dieter's staccato laughter felt like repeated slaps to his ears.

'Put his body in last. That way he'll be the first to go over the edge and less likely to be found.'

'Good thinking. I must say I do appreciate what you're doing for us.'

'Families need to stick together.'

'Yes, yes they do.'

CHAPTER 8

CLAIMING TO BE EAGER to get back to Krakow, Heinz refused lunch but accepted a food parcel to eat later. Magda's parents and the whole Hoffman brood came out to wave him goodbye. He roared up the street, ripped round the corner with brakes squealing like butchered pigs – and set off for home. The weather was excellent, and he kept driving fast with his window open.

The stink of rotting cabbages alerted him to the proximity of the dump. There was a wooden notice by the side of the road which indicated its municipal function. In reality, it was just a small ravine at the side of the road filling up with foul detritus.

He parked up and removed the stranger's body which let out a nauseating smell. His facial muscles were stiffening, but full rigor mortis had yet to set in, and Heinz manhandled him into the passenger seat, setting his feet down and placing his waxy hands on his lap. His eyes were already closed so a passer-by would assume he was having a nap.

It was hard work with an uncooperative corpse and sweat moistened his armpits and back. Disturbing sounds whistled and clanged in his ears. He tried to shake himself free of them without success. A car backfired in the distance, but nobody drove past. The smell of blood and death yanked him back to the trenches. Jumbled images of contorted faces, bloodied limbs, stiffened corpses whirled around him in a grotesque kaleidoscope. He squeezed his eyes shut and pinched the bridge of his nose. He forced himself back to the present and switched his mind to robot mode. Compassion would only hinder what he needed to do to survive.

By the time he had removed the remaining bodies, he was panting with the effort. One body had lodged near the top of the ravine. He grabbed the shovel and rammed muck and humus on top of it. He brought the stench of the dump back inside the cab and lost any desire for food. His senses wired, he was determined to break the back of the journey and discard the truck tonight. There were three potential sites near the farm where he knew careless drivers had careered to their deaths.

Stopping to refuel, he was heartened to see how much petrol he had left. He was making good time and soon passed Wolfgang and Elisabeth's farmhouse. Hunger now gnawed at his stomach; he stopped and tore a piece of bread to chew. Hunger would help him stay alert; he could always tuck into the remains of the food parcel later that night. As he approached the first site, he checked his mirror; there was nobody on the road behind him. Damn. Somebody had put up a sturdy barrier and painted white chevrons on the wooden rails. What if they had done the same at the next two sites?

He stopped the truck and shut down the engine. He would just have to hope for better luck; in any case, he wanted to be nearer the farm to reduce the distance he would have to walk. He took stock of the contents of the truck and found Henni's basket still in the back. He wouldn't go hungry, that was for sure, and there was a small bottle of Schnapps inside to toast his adventure, or should he say death. In the remaining daylight, he repacked his haversack and placed all the spare clothes in the cab to keep them warm.

Back on the road, he wondered at the premonition that had made him swap his suitcase and bring along his hiking stick. Perhaps Lady Luck was smiling at him? Well, whether she was or wasn't, he was going to make this work, even if it killed him. He chortled at his own wit and started whistling the popular tune, Erika, before bursting into song: 'On the heath, there blooms a little flower and it's called – he stamped his foot three times – Erika.'

The song's lyrics had his torso marching in his seat and he missed the second exit site. Shit. That was stupid. The light was fading, and he only had one more chance. Concentrate, Heinz, it's now or never. He found the third site, on a sharp bend in the road, and felt sick. He walked to the edge and peered down. The road had been banked up; he would have to pick up some speed, then brake in time to get his front wheel over the bank and pray it stayed there. He removed his possessions and placed them out of sight further up the road. If it went wrong, he would leap out and hope he was still alive to retrieve them. It was time. With clammy hands and cold sweats making him shiver, he climbed back into the cab. He reversed down the road, accelerated hard, and lurched forward before shrieking to a halt just beyond the bank. From the corner of his eye, he watched the corpse hit the windscreen with a thud.

'Yes, yes, yes.' He jumped out, turned his face to the night sky, and thanked his lucky stars. At the side of the cab, he pulled his companion out and then wedged him behind the wheel using brute force. Sorry, my friend, you didn't deserve any of this. He took out the remaining petrol cans and used one to soak the corpse from head to foot; the second one he poured over the mattress in the back.

A thought struck him, and he used the shovel to lever the number plate off the truck and threw it as far as he could down the hill. The sudden braking had created convincing ridges in the soil. Now the hard part. He reached over the soaking corpse and released the handbrake. He stepped back. Nothing happened. Shit, shit, shit. He should have risked it; he should have gone further; how the hell was he going to shift a ton of metal? Think, Heinz, think.

He could set light to it here, but that wouldn't convince anyone of a traffic accident. Wait a minute. Of course. He would have to start up the truck, let it roll and then leap out the way. Without the burst of speed, he needed to get over the bank, he should be able to launch himself free without too much trouble.

The petrol fumes were giving him a headache. He levered himself back into the cab, pushing the corpse onto its side. Did the position of the corpse matter? He moved it back and sat astride one knee, hunkered down. He turned the key and revved the engine while he gathered his courage. God help him: this had to work. He double declutched, put the truck into gear and gently pressed down the accelerator. The truck started to move and gather pace. For a split second, Heinz was tempted to stay with it. Then he thought of Henni and threw himself out. A tracery of branches and brambles scraped his face and clothes as he rolled to a halt. He sat up and watched the truck career down the hill, gathering speed until it hit something solid and burst into flames.

He wondered if any Allied bombers would be passing overhead, puzzled at a fire in the middle of nowhere. On balance, he thought it unlikely.

It was done. He should have been elated; instead, deep fatigue turned his bones into rubber. He could barely stagger up the incline. He was ashamed to find himself close to tears. In the cold night air, he changed his damp shirt and trousers and replaced his socks. He unscrewed the bottle of Schnapps and drank several draughts. He lifted the bottle in a silent toast to his dead doppelganger. He had used him, and he didn't even know his name. What kind of world did he live in? What kind of man had he become? He lurched forward, steadying himself on his stick, and headed down the road, searching for the narrow pathway that would lead him home. The moon was bright enough to let him see his way and eventually, his pounding heart calmed, and he looked for somewhere sheltered to sleep.

Daybreak saw him wake cold and stiff. His head throbbed from lack of water. His face was rough and sore. He chewed on some bread and set off. There was a stream somewhere near the footpath, but he didn't know the best way to get to it. He took out the map he'd borrowed from Gunter and tried to work out where he was. Perhaps he should just carry on? The sooner he got to the farm, the better. It would take him most of the day as it was. He trudged uphill and down, listening out for any passers-by, ready to hide before they saw him. He didn't want to stumble onto the farm unannounced and wondered where he could find Gunter. At long last he came to the padlocked gate marking the entrance to their farm; the Nazi flag hung from a tall wooden pole, tattered from the winds and rain. He ducked down as a car sped along the adjacent road. He climbed over the gate and plodded uphill. Head down and lost in his thoughts, he never noticed his father-in-law coming out of a side field.

'Heinz?'

'Gunter! Thank God I've bumped into you.'

In a rush, he explained everything he'd thought and done since leaving the farm. Gunter frowned, scratched his head and then watched, a bemused expression on his face, as legs gave way and Heinz toppled over.

'Here, let me help you up. It'll be getting dark shortly, so the children should be inside by now. I'll take you into the barn; then I'll come and fetch you once they're in bed and asleep. That way I can explain things to Henni before I come and fetch you. When did you last eat?'

'Today. I'm not hungry. I'm just desperate for some water.'

That night, seated around the table, the four of them talked and planned and worked out what to say to the children and to Lottie. After Gunter and Wanda had gone to bed, Henni heated water and made Heinz wash in front of the range.

'I can still smell that petrol on you.'

'Sorry.'

'I'll bring you down some pyjamas. If you leave the clothes outside, I'll wash them tomorrow.'

'Henni?'

'Yes?'

'Do you think I did the right thing?'

'Time will tell.'

It wasn't the answer he had been hoping to hear.

CHAPTER 9

ALP SAT IN THE den, his folded-up jacket creating a throne while he awaited his acolyte, or so it seemed to Heinz as he ducked inside the shelter. He handed over his offering of cheese and an apple. Alp nodded his thanks and tucked into the meal.

'The food situation is getting worse,' he said between mouthfuls. 'It's pitiful to see the hordes of children, orphans I should imagine, roaming the streets searching for anything useful to sell, begging for food, stealing when they get a chance.

'Not just children, of course. The adults are just as desperate but somehow less shocking. And they don't hunt in packs either. This is what they have reduced us to: our cities in ruins, rampant starvation and our oppressors strutting around proclaiming their great democracy. What a joke!

'And I can't tell you how disappointed I am with our fellow citizens. Do you remember those great rallies we had at the beginning? Thousands upon thousands cheering and celebrating our Fuehrer? They couldn't do enough for him: young men, old men, all full of pride, saluting him; women, tears in their eyes, desperate to have his blessing, to touch his hand, to do his every bidding.

'Now? Now, nobody was at those rallies; nobody agreed with the Fuehrer's policies; nobody wanted any part of National Socialism. As if that wasn't bad enough, they're all too quick to point the finger at anyone in authority. Oh yes, they say, he was a Nazi and good riddance to him. Me, Sir? No, Sir! I had nothing to do with any of it. It was all forced upon us.

'Hitler was right to be disappointed with the German people. They let him down. They didn't have it in them to fight to the bitter end and they don't have it in them now.'

Alp kicked at the banked soil; fungal motes spread in the air; the sudden smell of decay caught in their throats, and they looked away from each other.

'Any beer?'

Heinz nodded towards the corner of the den but didn't move. What was he doing here? What was the point of it all? He wasn't going to become a Werewolf; he wasn't even sure he wanted Alp's company anymore. He'd come expecting to be distracted and now Alp had plunged him back into the misery caused by Hitler's stupid war and his stupid refusal to surrender. He closed his eyes and longed for an end to the thoughts battering his brain. He'd been happy once; was he never to be happy again?

'Mind if I have your beer as well? It's thirsty work climbing up to your den.'

Heinz shrugged his shoulders in reply. In the distance, he heard the dogs barking and vaguely wondered what had upset them. He needed to get up but lacked the energy. He'd told Gunther he would help him mend some fences in the far field that afternoon. From where he was sitting, slouched against the mossy bank, it seemed a mammoth undertaking.

'Thank God our people can still rely on us,' said Alp. 'Meine Ehre Heisst Treue – My Honour is Loyalty. Always was, always will be.'

'What do you mean?'

'We've come up with a plan.'

A grin spread across Heinz's face. He might have guessed Alp wouldn't be deterred by the moral failure of the German people.

'Tell me more.'

'We need an underground railroad: an escape route for our war heroes to leave Germany and find safety abroad. The Werewolves can help to provide food and shelter; they can also act as guides through dangerous or difficult terrain. No hero will be abandoned or lacking in support. Even the Werewolves who've lost heart and returned home will help their comrades-in-arms.

'These are our brothers, Heinz. We cannot let them down in their hour of need. You're isolated up here; you've no idea what life is like under the occupiers. People were terrified of being overrun by the Red Army, but do not fondly imagine that we're any better off under the Americans or the British. Hundreds of thousands of soldiers and civilians are being held in camps in appalling conditions. You were a soldier in the Great War, weren't you? You know a soldier's role in life and in death. It's not to question the rights or wrongs of war; that's a job for politicians. You're there to do your duty, to obey your commanding officer and to support fellow soldiers.

'Earlier this month, two of our Werewolves, mere youngsters, were executed by firing squad for spying on American forces. If that's happening in American territories, it doesn't take much imagination to work out what's happening in the Soviet zone. We've intercepted reports that talk of thousands being liquidated. Liquidated! It hurts me here when I see a word like that, Heinz, as if we're lice instead of human beings.

'We must do everything we can to bring our brothers to safety. You can see that, can't you?'

'Yes, yes I can.'

He thought back to the trenches of the Great War. All those soldiers thrown together in terrible circumstances were brothers at heart. Sitting there, cleaning his gun, he'd watched the camaraderie play out in front of him. A helping hand, a kind word, even a joke was all that kept them going back then.

Alp was right: he was isolated up here. Who knew what reprisals the Americans would want to carry out? He wasn't an evil man; he didn't deserve to languish in jail; he didn't deserve to die. Incarcerated in an Allied camp, he would want an escape plan, buddies to help him get away and start a new life. He thought of Henni and his children.

'What about their families?'

'We've thought of that. It all depends on circumstances. Some can get away with their wives and children immediately; some families will have to wait until their loved ones have reached safety and then we will help to reunite them. It'll all take time, but that's something we're not short of.'

'I can't tell my family about this or involve them.'

'You don't need to.'

'And this isn't my territory. I'm a Berlin man, born and bred. I could guide you through a city landscape; out here I'm lost.'

'You'd be lost in our cities now, especially Berlin. There's nothing left but rubble and more rubble. Sometimes it's hard to work out where one street ends and another begins. Have you ever seen the moon through a telescope? No? Well, I thought of that eerie desert of mountains and craters when I walked through Munich the other day. It was so sad to witness.'

'So, what do you want me to do?'

'Keep this den stocked up with food and water. It's been well made, I'm glad to say, so it's dry and comfortable. Perhaps you could bring a blanket to sleep on in case anybody has to shelter overnight? Do you have a metal container to keep the food in? We don't want to attract any animals.'

'There's a small one buried on the other side of the beer. We keep some smoked sausage in it.'

Alp's eyes lit up. His fists clenched and unclenched as he battled with himself.

'Good, yes, good. German smoked sausage for our German heroes. An excellent choice.'

He sounded like a snooty waiter in an expensive restaurant; Heinz felt sorry for him and changed the subject.

'Where will they go from here?'

'Anyone passing this way will head over the Alps into Austria, then Italy. The Vatican is very helpful to our cause and we're building up a network of

Catholic priests. They don't want the world overrun by communists any more than we do. Say what you like about the Third Reich, it offered the world stability; the communists will tear the heart and soul out of every man, woman, and child they enslave in their system.'

'What about the Protestants?'

'I don't know. I expect they hate communism too, but they're not getting a steer from the top the way the Catholics are.'

'When do you want me to start?'

'I'll be back as soon as I can. Wait for my signal.'

'Alp?'

'Yes?'

'How did you find out about me? Was it Obersturmbannfuehrer Hoffman who contacted you? And do you know what happened to him?'

'He's your brother-in-law, isn't he? No, I'll ask around for you, but I haven't heard anything and, no, he didn't contact us. The Gauleiter had files on all the families with notes on who was loyal, who was suspect. That was our starting point for new recruits. The funny thing was your file had "Deceased" stamped on it. Guess there must have been some clerical error.'

'Must have been. So why did you come after me?'

'Pure chance. I was checking out hiding places in the forest when I saw you. Followed you down to the farm, found out who it belonged to and put two and two together.'

Heinz returned to the farm in a pensive mood. The ruse had worked, at least until Alp came along. To think he had spent all those months living in fear of being hunted down as a traitor when nobody knew of his existence. If the Americans had access to the same files – and why wouldn't they, now they were the occupying power? – then he was safe from them too. The knowledge should have put a spring in his step; instead, he was wary of what he didn't know. Where was Albrecht? Was he still a danger? Did Henni still want to kill her brother?

'Papa, we saw Jesse Owens.'

'Yes, Papa, we did, we did, we did.'

What new children's game was this? Carola and Tomas were holding hands and spinning in a circle, shouting the name repeatedly. Even Monika was clapping her hands to the rhythm of the name. He shook his head with an indulgent smile and went indoors. Henni sat at the table, holding her head in her hands, a snapshot of misery. Lottie was rocking from side to side, her rheumy eyes large with incomprehension.

'What on earth's happened? You look beaten down.'

'They came. The Americans. Two soldiers and an interpreter.'

'Did they hurt you?'

'No, they were very polite.'

'What then?'

'They requisitioned most of the larder.'

'Oh.' Her pride and joy ransacked. No wonder she looked so glum.

'You poor thing, Henni. I'm so sorry you had to deal with that on your own. I should have been here.' He hugged his wife and felt a tremulous joy as she leaned into him.

'Thank God you weren't here. They would only

have taken you away for questioning and then where would we be?'

'They didn't find the second larder?'

'No! Thank the Lord, they didn't even think to look.' Her eyes lit up as she clasped her hands to her chest.

When Heinz first returned to the farm, he helped Gunter build a false wall at the back of the lean-to. The access point was cleverly concealed. Together, they identified other hiding places around the farm and inside the house. The main larder always looked well stocked to put people off looking for other supplies. Their careful planning had paid off.

'Did they meet Gunter?'

'No, at least I don't think so. I suppose they could have bumped into him on their way out. I don't know what his plans were for the day.'

'And Wanda?'

'She hid upstairs in your hideaway. I thought it was better that way.'

As Gunter walked in, Lottie gurgled with pleasure and lifted her arms like a toddler wanting to be picked up. He knelt by her chair and listened to Henni describe their visitors.

'One of them was black. All chewing that stuff, what's it called? Gum. The black one blew an enormous bubble with it. When it popped, I thought the children's eyes would pop out.' She half smiled at the memory.

'They even offered the children some, but I declined on their behalf. Then Monika asked, "Are you Jesse Owens, the fastest man in the world?" That made them all roar with laughter, except for the interpreter who was a pompous little man. I was at school with him. I can't recall his name, but you'd know him, Papa, if you saw him. Anyway, he was much too important to acknowledge me, let alone help me. "People are starving in the cities, Mrs Bauer. We must all do what we can to help and share our resources." I bet he was a Nazi too, just like that officious block warden we had in Berlin. Do you remember him, Heinz?

'I kept asking them to leave us enough to feed the family, but when they asked how many we were, I only told them about Gunter. I didn't even mention Wanda. So, of course, they didn't think we needed that much.'

Supper that night was a subdued affair. The children had exhausted themselves and sat eating; the adults were absorbed in their own thoughts and speculations. Heinz considered how much food he could squirrel away with the diminished supplies; a canny housekeeper like Henni would soon notice gaps in the larder.

He was at peace with himself. Henni had accepted his hug and then she'd chatted away, just like old times. He would tell her. Why not? Bring her in on his secret mission. She would understand his desire to help his fellow soldiers. Hadn't she lost her own brothers in the last war and cried bitter tears of grief? She would understand the importance of camaraderie, of reaching out a helping hand.

He would suggest a stock take, just the two of them wandering around the house and barn, assessing what they had and what they could spare. He imagined her puzzled face: what do you mean, Heinz, what we can spare? What's going on? And he would tell her everything, everything about Alp, about the camps, about helping the war heroes escape. He wouldn't mention the Werewolves; no need to muddy the waters with that nonsense. They were all just soldiers escaping rough justice meted out by the Allies. After all, they couldn't expect mercy after Hitler had forced them to fight to the end.

He helped put the children to bed, read them stories until their eyes were closing, and then retired to their bedroom.

'I'll be up shortly,' she said.

He stretched out in the bed, a fuzzy warmth spreading through his limbs, and he fell asleep dreaming of happier times when they'd talked and laughed and solved all their problems together.

CHAPTER 10

'Heinz, wake up. Lottie has gone missing.'

Startled awake, he pulled on his clothes.

'What time is it?'

'Just gone five. Gunter's out bringing in the cows for milking. He doesn't know she's gone.'

'Could she have gone with him?'

'No, he would have left a note.'

'Right, where do you want me to search?'

'Start around the farm and then head down the track to the gate. She's been talking a lot about her friend Karin. Perhaps she's taken it into her head to visit her? Lord, this is all we need.'

'Don't worry, Henni, we'll find her. She can't have gone far.'

'I'd better stop here. I don't want any of the children waking up and finding there's nobody around.'

Heinz checked the farm buildings, calling out Lottie's name wherever he went. Rumbustious birds twittered and cheeped all around him in the trees. He breathed in the air, relishing its purity. He strode down the shaded path; the early morning dew glistened on the grass and highlighted myriad cobwebs. A deep and restful sleep had revived his mind and body. He felt a glorious oneness with everything around him. Life was good, and it was going to get even better. He had a purpose, a noble one, and soon he would have his wife alongside him, facing the future as one.

'Lottieeee.'

The birds continued to chatter; something rustled in the undergrowth; farther away a larger animal crashed through the bushes.

'Lottieeee.'

She lay ahead of him, spreadeagled, motionless.

'Oh, God. Lottie, Lottie, can you hear me?'

There was a gash on her head where she'd hit a stone on the path; it didn't look too serious. She felt cold to the touch, which concerned him more. He worried about moving her, but what choice did he have? She moaned without opening her eyes as he gathered her into his arms and carried her back to the farmhouse.

Henni stood in the open doorway, keeping a lookout, and ran towards him.

'I'll take her straight upstairs. We need to get this damp nightie off her and wrap her in blankets. She's breathing but she's not waking up.'

Henni grabbed a fresh nightie and together they made her comfortable.

'I'll get a basin of warm water to clean up her wound.'

'Thanks, Heinz, I don't want to leave her.'

The morning passed like treacle dripping off a wooden spoon. Gunter's face aged with every hour; he carried on his farm work like a man lost, checking regularly on Lottie; only Tomas, trying manfully to keep up with

Gunter's long strides brought an occasional smile to his face. The children rose to the occasion: Carola refused to leave Lottie's side while Monika busied herself in the kitchen helping Wanda prepare their meals.

Surplus to requirements, Heinz wandered into the kitchen garden, picked up Wanda's hoe and started weeding where she'd left off. How quickly things could change. He'd made a breakthrough with Henni, he was certain of it, and now this. Perhaps he wasn't as lucky as he'd assumed. He finished the row and moved across to his section, where he spotted two figures of eight laid out in small stones. Another game? No. The children knew how important the garden was to their family's survival and never ventured there on their own, and never to play. How stupid could he be? It was a sign from Alp. He wished he would stop using Heil Hitler, but it wasn't worth an argument. How long had it been there? There was only one way to find out; he kicked over the stones and set off for the den.

He touched the ground; it was still warm where Alp normally sat. He couldn't have been gone long. He stepped outside and leant against a spruce. If Alp was anywhere in the vicinity, he would come back. Heinz was sure of that.

'Papa, help me.' His son's scream sent ice down his spine. Where was he? Where did the scream come from?

'Let my son go or I swear to God, I'll kill you with my bare hands.' His furious roar vibrated in the air.

Tomas was hanging in the air, his shirt caught in Alp's iron grip, another hand raised to strike him. Heinz ran towards them, stumbling over roots, steadying himself on trunks, distraught at the tears tumbling down his son's cheeks.

'You're hurting him. Let him go right now, or everything ends. I mean it, Alp.'

Narrowed eyes flashed, a look of such cruelty that Heinz's mouth gaped open. This time he spoke in a gentle voice.

'Let him down, Alp, then we'll talk.' He walked towards them.

'The little spy. He needs to be taught a lesson he won't forget. You need to thrash him and thrash him hard.' He shook the boy in emphasis.

'I am his father, Alp. Let him go.' Slow, calm, authoritative words.

'Yes, you are right. That is your duty, not mine. Here, take him.' He dropped Tomas, who ran and wrapped himself around his father's legs.

Heinz bent down and wiped the tears from his son's face.

'It's all right, son.'

'I wasn't doing anything wrong, Papa. I came to tell you Oma is feeling better.'

'That's splendid news, Tomas. I'll be down to see Oma in a while. Now you go back home. Do you know the way? Good boy.'

'Good boy?' The scorn gave an ugly twist to his mouth.

'What are you, Heinz, a man or a mouse? We didn't build the Glorious Third Reich on the back of weak parenting. Without discipline there is no obedience; without obedience there is chaos.

'My earliest memory is bent over my father's knee. A slipper until I was seven and then it was his belt. I had to kiss his hand afterwards and thank him. "Thank you, Father, for teaching me the right way to behave." His word was law, and I respected him with every fibre of my being. He made me the man I am today.

'And don't tell me your father was any different because I won't believe you. Every father worth his name has instilled discipline in his children from time immemorial.'

His face betrayed a complex array of emotions: a superior smirk as he stared straight at him, chin upturned, eyebrow raised, then the features collapsing, cheeks flushed as he passed a hand over his eyes and swallowed hard.

'I was eighteen the last time he beat me. I'd been out smoking with my friends and a neighbour, Mr Neumann, Karl Neumann, saw me. He told my father, who called me into his study. "Don't be too hard on him," Neumann said as he left. My father just looked at me and jerked his head towards the door. I went upstairs to my bedroom and waited for my punishment. I never touched another cigarette after that.'

Heinz didn't know what to say. His own father had never beaten him, and he couldn't imagine finding it in himself to inflict pain on his beloved son. It wasn't that he had never been naughty as a child or disobedient. A broken ornament came to mind, its fragments spread across the parquet floor. His mother's anger still rankled, but what he remembered most of all was the disappointment in his father's face. A disappointment that still had the power to cause him pain and regret today.

His instinct, his son's instinct, surely all human instinct, was to seek protection and love from your parents. What effect did it have on a man to have that basic trust battered from an early age? But Alp was right: most of his childhood friends had grown up knowing the sting of a switch or a belt administered by their father. It guaranteed a lot of respect, but perhaps not so much love. And without love? Without love, we were all lost.

Staring through Alp, he saw the massed ranks of Nazi automatons, expressionless faces, arms raised in salute: men whose instinct for love and caring had been beaten out of them as they thanked their father for teaching them the right way to behave. No wonder none of them could stand up to Hitler, to tell the most warped individual among them that this was all wrong and then, as the war was ending, that enough was enough, and it was time to surrender. A cough brought him back to the forest.

'I'm sorry, Alp, we're all at sixes and sevens today. My mother-in-law had a fall this morning and we've all been worried sick about her. I haven't even got any food to offer you.'

'Another time. We're all set to go. The first railroaders will come your way in a day or two. Just make sure there's food and water in the den.'

'Yes, of course.'

'I'll be off then.' He seemed reluctant to leave.

'Alp, how did you manage to leave the sign without setting off the dogs?'

Face lit up, he started whistling the family's secret tune. Heinz lifted his arms in a gesture of defeat. He wouldn't want to have Alp as an enemy, he thought, as he ambled back down to the farm.

CHAPTER 11

Fury was etched into Henni's face as she rushed forward like a woman possessed.

'What the hell are you playing at? How dare you risk our lives like that? How could you do that to me?'

Her voice escalated from a hiss to a harsh cry as she stomped towards Heinz and pushed him away again and again with a violence he'd never witnessed before.

'Henni, calm down.' He grabbed hold of her hand, but she wrenched it away.

'Don't ever tell me to calm down. And don't ever grab my hand like that. How dare you? Who the hell is he? Some tramp chancing his arm? What does he want? Don't tell me he's someone you've invited here.'

'No, look it's not like that.'

'Not like what? Don't you understand anything? Don't you know what times we live in? Bad enough that you endanger me but our children, Heinz? Our children? Have you any idea how terrified Tomas was?'

'Henni, please, this isn't helping. We need to talk.'

'Talk? No, Heinz, we're not going to talk about this. We're never going to talk about this. What you're going to do is make that man go away and never come back. Do you understand? It's fine for you to go and hide in your little den whenever there's any danger but you've no thought for me or for our children. I still can't believe you could do that to me. What on earth were you thinking?'

'Right, I've had enough of this. I've tried and tried to talk to you, to get through to you, but all you do is reject me.' Now it was his voice climbing up the scale to a crescendo of outrage.

'We used to share everything...'

'Oh, for God's sake, you stupid man. You don't understand anything, do you?' A sob rose from her stomach, breaking her voice.

'I was raped, Heinz. Tell me how I share that with you?' She turned on her heel and ran.

Her words came like a punch to the solar plexus; he staggered back, turning his head this way and that. Who? When? Why?

He sank to the ground, hiding his head in his hands.

'Get up, Heinz.'

'Go away, Wanda.'

'No, you listen to me.' Wanda's voice was as sharp as an axe splintering his armour. 'Henni needs you, not your self-pity, not your wounded male pride, but her husband, her protector, the man who can heal her wounds and make her feel human again. And she needs that now, not when you feel up to it.'

In that instant, he hated her for saying it but knew she was right.

'Where did she go?'

'Across the fields. My guess is Lisle's grave.'

He half walked and half ran to catch her up. His thoughts were black, murderous. He wanted revenge.

If he could lay his hands on the perpetrator, he would string him up himself. All thoughts of investigations or fair trials vanished in the force of his passion. The bastard. He spoke the words out loud, again and again. She was ahead of him in the distance, but he thought better of calling out to her. Then she disappeared behind a line of trees. He slowed down. What was he going to say? How could he ease her pain? Should he put his arm around her or keep a respectful distance? Would she welcome his presence or push him away? And if she pushed him away, how could he overcome that? He'd dealt with a few rape cases in his time, established trust with the victims, but this was his wife, dammit. He had no idea how to act around her.

She was sitting by Lisle's grave with her back to him. He semi-circled around her and placed a single cornflower on Lisle's grave.

'It'll die without water.'

'I know.' He sat down and waited.

'I'm so, so sorry Henni. I don't know if you want to talk or if there is anything I can do to ease your pain. Whatever you want me to do, I will do it.'

The silence continued for many minutes before Henni started to speak in a voice so quiet he had to lean towards her to hear her words.

'There were two of them. Thin, almost as thin as Wanda when she first came to us. Filthy clothes hanging off them, raddled faces, black fingernails. Their breath stank like a cesspit. We only had one guard dog at the time, and it was barking furiously. I looked out the window. One was pointing a gun. The next minute, the dog was dead. I locked the door, put a chair against the handle, but I didn't stand a chance.

'They used the bench outside as a battering ram. One of them pinned my arms behind my back. I tried to struggle free, but he pressed his gun against my neck and pushed me against the table.'

Her face crumpled into a gargoyle of pain. Tears cascaded down her cheeks. He moved closer and knelt at her side. Great sobs racked her body. She wiped away the snot. Red-rimmed, swollen eyes turned to look at him. Her nose blocked, she breathed through her mouth, her sentences coming out as awkwardly as hiccoughs.

'They had some German. The one raping me kept saying, "This is for my family...this is for my home...this is for my country." It went on and on. It wasn't natural. The pain was indescribable.'

She paused. 'I thought I would die.'

Heinz wiped away his own tears and reached for her hand. Her fingernails were bitten to the quick. How had he not noticed that before? She held his hand in her lap and continued. 'The other one had raided the larder and sat at the table watching while he stuffed his face, smacking loudly with every mouthful, adding his comments in a language I didn't recognize.

'Now and then, he'd get up and get himself something else to eat. Whatever he didn't fancy, he smashed to the ground. When it was over, I sank to the ground and curled up like a baby. All I wanted was my mother, my poor demented mother who was oblivious to it all, having her afternoon nap in bed. Snoring while her daughter was being raped.

'But I thank God for that small mercy. I could not have borne it if they'd attacked her as well.'

She blew her nose, her handkerchief sodden.

'Do you know what that does to a woman? Do you have any idea of the humiliation? I tried not to be there, to go elsewhere in my mind, but my body was still there, taking the abuse, taking the pain. I didn't care what he'd been through. He had no right to do that. I wasn't Hitler or even a Nazi. I was just a wife and mother, doing the best I could. I didn't care about any of it, not about a Thousand Year Reich or any of that stupid nonsense. I just wanted to bring up my children and live an ordinary life.

'He was a beast, Heinz. I can still hear his accented German in my ears. I can still smell his breath. Sometimes I can't bear to sit at the table with all of you, knowing what happened there. If anybody munches their food too loudly it brings it all rushing back; it makes mealtimes an agony.'

She shuddered. 'If I'd got hold of his gun, I would have shot him, and the other one, just to make sure but, as time passed, as the physical pain subsided, I grew to understand, yes, he was a beast, but we made him into that beast. You and I and all the rest of us.'

He frowned, puzzled by her words. 'But…'

'No, listen, Heinz. Those men were prisoners, forced labourers, and they were starving. Starving in our country and we did nothing about it. We were silent, you and I and all the rest of us.

'We lost sight of what it meant to be human. We became less than human, like stones or rocks, something beyond feeling, beyond hope, beyond redemption.'

'No, Henni, that's not true. What choice did we have? Surrounded by fanatics who would kill us if we stood up to them? Maybe we should have talked more, did more, but we didn't become rocks or stones. We did the best we could in circumstances beyond our control.'

She shook her head. 'No, Heinz, no. We didn't do what was right. It's as simple as that. I'm not making excuses for those men. What they did was evil, just as evil as anything the Nazis did. They didn't see me as a human being. They saw me as an object, something to abuse and discard. Our silence, our failure to do what was right, does not excuse or justify their behaviour. It's just that I see a connection between what we failed to do and their failure to be human because I don't see how you can be human and do that to another living being.'

'I understand some of what you are saying, but surely you are overthinking the situation. We have to be responsible for our own actions, of course. But we can't link what we've done or not done to whatever somebody else is doing or not doing. It doesn't work like that.'

'Perhaps.' Her face and tone were unconvinced. 'There's more I want to talk to you about, so much more I want to say, but not now. I need to pull myself together and get back to the farm.'

'You don't need to do anything, Henni. Stay here for as long as you like. I'll stay with you, if you like, or leave you in peace and move further away, whatever you want. Wanda has everything under control, so you don't have to hurry back.'

'Well, maybe I'll stop for longer. Besides, you need to tell me about this man.'

'Oh, Henni, it's a long story and I don't have the energy for it right now. The very last thing I want to do is belittle what you suffered, but this has completely knocked me off balance. A man wants to protect his wife and to know I didn't do that is shattering. Please trust me when I tell you he's no threat to you or to the children.'

'Humph, tell that to Tomas. He was terrified when he returned to the farm.'

'I'm sorry. Poor Tomas. I'll talk to him and the girls. He's just someone who uses the den from time to time, so it's best they don't go up there. Anyway, I'll tell you all about it another day.'

CHAPTER 12

Shadows were lengthening as they walked back to the farm, arm in arm. After whistling to the dogs, Heinz turned to his wife, lifted her hand, and kissed it.

'Please don't shut me out. I promise never to touch you until you are ready, until you want me to.'

Her eyes avoided his. 'What if that never happens?'

'Oh, Henni. What can I say? If it never happens, it never happens. You're still my beloved wife. I would do anything to make you happy and if that means sacrificing my own desires then so be it.'

She nodded.

'We can still hug, though, can't we?'

In response, she placed her arms around him, head on his shoulder. The embrace lasted several minutes until Monika walked out and scowled at them.

'Oma's been calling for you.' She turned back inside and shut the door on them.

'I haven't cracked that one yet.'

Henni smiled. 'No, she's a tough nut.'

They parted and Heinz headed for the milking shed where the cows were being released to go back into their field.

'Papa!'

'Tomas, I have a very important job for you. I'm going to help Opa take the cows, and while we're doing that, I want you to pick some flowers for Mama. Some special flowers to make her happy and smile a great big smile. Do you know the blue cornflowers that grow along the way? Good, pick a handful of those, mind you don't squash them, and then we'll all walk back together.'

Tomas ran off, eyes bright and questing.

'I wish you'd told me, Gunter.'

'I couldn't. She made me swear on all that was dear to me not to tell a soul, not even you, maybe especially not you. She was in such a bad way that I didn't hesitate to agree. At that moment, I would have done literally anything to relieve her distress.

'It's strange how people always think a man wants to have sons to carry on the family name, how they even commiserate with you when a daughter is born, but I never felt that way. When Henni was born I was over the moon, and I felt so protective towards her. She was so tiny, so delicate, so trusting. When I first held her in my arms, my heart melted and I cried, partly with joy, partly with this tremendous sense of responsibility for her.

'I would have done anything for her then, and I would do anything for her now. I'm sorry, Heinz, sorry for what happened to her, sorry I wasn't there to protect her, sorry for what it's done to both of you.'

He paused to smack a wayward cow on the rump, his voice low and grumbling. 'Get on with you. Go on.'

'Where were the children?'

'They were with me, thank God. I'd taken them and Wanda to visit our neighbours. You haven't met Hans and Clara yet, have you? Hans is a man of few words and I think the children find him a bit frightening, but his wife, Clara, is warm and welcoming. She and Wanda had a rapport with each other from the moment they first met and when they invited her to visit as well as the children, Henni absolutely insisted that she should go.

'She kept saying it would do her good to have a break from the farm and Clara picked up on that and invited her to stay for a few days saying they would happily bring her back the following week. Perhaps it was for the best. The intruders were armed so Wanda couldn't have done anything to help Henni and it probably saved her from the same fate.

'Anyway, the arrangements were made and on the given day we set off in good spirits never imagining...' his voice trailed off. He took a sharp intake of breath. 'Their own children are grown up now, but they've kept all their toys and books, so it was like an Aladdin's cave for the little ones, and they had the most wonderful time.

'We stopped there for something to eat and afterwards the children were allowed to choose one toy or book each to take back home. You can imagine how thrilled they were: Christmas had come early. They were chattering away to each other as we walked back, and I was in a world of my own.

'It was Monika who stopped me in my tracks. "Opa, the dog isn't barking." I had a sudden sense of foreboding. They knew we had the dog to protect us from bad men who might try to steal something from us, so I was able to persuade them to hide together in the woods and wait there until I returned for them.

'I ran down to the farm. The dog was a bloody mess, and I threw my jacket over him, in case the children disobeyed me and saw him. The door lock was smashed, the bench lying to one side. My heart was in my mouth as I stepped inside. Henni was lying on the floor crying. The place was a mess, with broken jars and food all over the place.

'That was the moment Lottie came downstairs. I imagine she'd finished her afternoon nap. Anyway, she was comparatively lucid and became terribly upset seeing her kitchen so untidy and so much wasted food. She always hated wasting food. She was waving her arms around like a lunatic octopus. It was horrible to watch.

'She kept asking "What's happened here? What have you done in my kitchen? What have you done to my stores?" It was laughable, really, because she's taken no interest in the kitchen or the stores for months. I didn't know what to say. I didn't want to upset her with talk of intruders, so I blurted out, "It's those damned foxes. They've run riot in here. I'm going to have to shoot them, Lottie." And God bless her, that seemed to satisfy her. "Naughty foxes," she said, sat down in my chair and started singing "Fox, you stole the Goose." She sang the whole song over and over again, which enabled me to start cleaning up and made sure that damned tune is stuck in my head for ever more.

'I couldn't leave the children for too long so I told Henni what I would say to them, and suggested she went upstairs to lie down. I offered to sort out supper and everything else. She agreed with the story but said she would stay up until she'd seen them to stop them worrying. She was so amazingly brave about it all.'

'So, what did you say to the children?'

'The dog had died of old age. Mama wasn't feeling well and foolish Opa had broken the lock when it jammed, and he had to push hard against it.'

'Did they believe you?'

'They went along with it. It helped that Monika had noticed some grey hairs in the dog's coat, so we chatted about grey hair and how mine was still dark, but Oma's had gone white even though she's younger than me. Then Monika told Tomas his hair would go white because he was younger than she was and Tomas said it wouldn't because he was a farmer like Opa, so it would stay dark.

'It would all have been funny and charming if only my heart wasn't broken from seeing Henni so devastated. But, like I said, she was amazingly brave. She was waiting at the open door with a biscuit barrel in her hand and glasses of milk on the table and the children showed her their gifts and told her all about their day. You wouldn't know anything had happened.

'While they were having their snack, I buried the dog. It's so sad because, if it wasn't for the children and for Lottie's dementia, the guard dog would have been running loose and none of this would have happened. I did a makeshift repair on the lock until I had time to replace it. I also made sure, and believe me, I feel so guilty I didn't do this before, that she has easy access to one of my shotguns. She keeps it hidden in the broom cupboard. It's always loaded, which worries me because of the children, but there's a latch on the door out of their reach.

'As the days passed, I thought of more and more security measures: internal shutters for the windows; wooden bars to place across the door; a chain to fix the bench to the wall. I was becoming obsessed, and it was all too late for Henni. Still, it gave me the idea for a second larder and other useful hiding places.'

'Do you know what happened to the men?'

'Not really. I told Henni the militia had caught two escaped prisoners and hung them because I thought it would give her peace of mind.'

'Did it?'

'No. I found her reaction quite strange. She said, "Another two lives wasted." They would have been more than wasted if I'd got my hands on them.'

'You and me together.'

'Incidentally, what's this Tomas tells me about a bad man in the forest?'

'It's all right; he's not a danger to Tomas or anyone else. He's just someone who uses the den from time to time. I guess I've kind of befriended him and in turn, he gives me news of the outside world, which I miss.

'He says there's terrible poverty and homelessness and starvation in the cities. Children running wild. Rubble and destruction everywhere. Dead bodies still visible in the ruins. We were all so terrified of the Russian invasion that we didn't stop to think what life might be like under the British or the Americans. And, apparently, it's not good.'

'No, well, that's what war does to the defeated. I don't suppose there's been a war in any part of the world or in any century you care to name that hasn't brought terrible suffering in its wake, some of it deliberate like the violence and destruction, some of it a by-product like starvation and homelessness. If we'd surrendered earlier, there wouldn't be so much destruction to contend with.

'I'm sure there are both good and bad men among the Allies, but I do have a certain sympathy for their commanders. It can't be easy to try and restore order to the chaos. Just trying to distribute food fairly must be a nightmare even if they manage to get sufficient supplies.

'We're lucky to be up here, away from the worst of it, but I'm sure those Americans will be back for more food. I hope they've got the sense to leave the cows alone. Far better to donate all our milk and cheese than lose the means of production.'

'Killing the goose that lays the golden eggs.'

'Exactly.'

'Papa, look.' Tomas came running up, waving a handful of cornflowers.

'Careful now. The stems are delicate. If you wave them around too much, they'll break. Gunter, we'll head back down if that's all right with you. I want to talk to Tomas.'

Tomas looked up at his father with wary eyes. 'It's nothing to worry about, son. I wanted to talk to you about the man in the forest.'

'The bad man.'

'He's not bad, Tomas, although he was very wrong to threaten you like that.'

'I think he's bad.'

'Well, I don't want to argue. He's using my den for a while.'

'Why?'

'Because he doesn't have a home of his own, because of all the bombs that fell during the war.'

'Oh.'

'Is that all right? For him to use the den?'

'Suppose.'

'I know you came to tell me the good news about Oma, but I think it would be better if you didn't go up to the den again. At least not while he's there. Will you stay away from there?'

'Yes, Papa.'

'Good and I'll tell the girls to stay away as well.'

CHAPTER 13

HEINZ KNELT ON AN old sack stuffed with straw as he planted pumpkin seeds in a neat row. On the other side of the garden, Wanda busied herself bringing out tomato plants in pots ready to plant out. She was singing to herself, a pleasant tune Heinz didn't recognize; when she walked past him, he caught snatches of words that sounded foreign and yet familiar. Mid-morning, Henni brought out three coffees, and they sat together, enjoying the sun's warmth.

'It would be nice for Lottie to come and sit in the garden. Carola is keeping her company, but she wants to go and help Gunther with the bees. The sun will do Lottie good, and I'll be able to get on with the housework without keeping an eye on her. She won't be too much of a bother, will she?'

'We'll manage if she is. Do you want me to fetch her chair?'

Minutes later, Lottie was ensconced in her rocker, a straw hat shielding her face, and a blanket covering her thin legs. She moved her arms, conducting a secret orchestra and then just as suddenly fell asleep. Wanda waved to catch his attention and pointed.

'I wasn't sure she would make it after her fall,' said Heinz.

'No? The old can be tougher than they look. I learnt that in the camp.'

'How long were you there for?'

'Six months before I was selected for nanny duties.'

'Magda told me you are a Jehovah's Witness. I must admit I don't know much about them.'

'Neither do I.'

'Pardon?'

'I'm Jewish.'

'What?'

'Close your mouth, Heinz, it makes you look stupid, if you don't mind me saying so.'

'Oh, right.'

He stood stock still, feeling as stupid as he'd looked. Was nothing as it seemed? How many more surprises were going to be thrown at him like balls at a coconut shy? He looked at Wanda with fresh interest. She didn't look at all Jewish, but that wasn't surprising; only an idiot would have fallen for those propaganda posters of evil Jews with their hooked noses, green faces, and malevolent red eyes. And yet, people did.

'That song you were singing earlier on, was it Yiddish?'

'No, it's a Polish lullaby. I used to sing it to Peter.'

'Will you tell me your story?'

'I'm happy to if you get on with some work as well. I'm not carrying on gardening while you just stand there listening. Honestly, why can't men do two things at once?'

Heinz felt his mouth open again and closed it. Their relationship was going to differ greatly from now on.

'In that case, I suggest we both get on with planting seeds in the same bed.'

As they knelt, each busy with their own tasks, Wanda related her journey from ghetto to safe house to betrayal to Auschwitz. She spoke without emotion as if the person whose trials she was describing was somebody different. The sun was beating down on them and Wanda went to fetch a sun hat.

Despite the heat, Heinz shivered; heavy limbs made his movements slow and lumbering. Instead of Wanda's returning figure, he saw the ghosts of thousands of Jewish men, women, and children he'd helped to round up in Berlin. The brutality, the random acts of cruelty, the outright sadism she'd described had their echo in his own experiences.

Each night he'd tried to drown out the sights and sounds with liberal quantities of Schnapps and Beethoven's 5th Symphony played so loud the neighbours complained. It hadn't worked; in the end, he had to make a conscious effort to put it all behind him when he returned to his normal duties, but the images remained lodged in his brain.

'The cattle trucks they used for our transport stank, unfortunately not of cattle. It was an acrid smell that grabbed the back of your throat. They kept loading more and more people into the same truck. It was impossible to move or even breathe. Somebody further back panicked, screamed, and tried to force their way out. I heard a slap and then quiet weeping. I'll never understand why we didn't jump out and run for it. They couldn't shoot all of us, not all at once anyway. I guess hope is the last thing to die. We thought we'd just put up with this and then there might be something better at the end.

'I was one of the last ones on and then they tried to thrust another woman on. "She's not one of us," said a man next to me, but he helped me pull her on, anyway. "I doubt that matters where we're going," I said, and we both looked at each other. We all knew it wasn't going to end well whatever we tried to tell ourselves.

'The poor woman was bleeding from the side of her head. She leant against me, past caring. At some point during the night, I could feel she was dead. Quite a few died during that journey. There was nothing to do, so I started wondering about her, what kind of life she'd led, why she'd come to their attention. Then it occurred to me that I could become her. It was a risk, of course, but being Jewish wasn't going to help me survive. Perhaps she would.

'I managed to extricate my arm – we were so jammed together it was hard work – and bit by bit I went through her pockets until I found her papers. And that's how I became Wanda Janowska, Jehovah's Witness.

'Whether it was luck or God's guiding hand or whatever, as soon as I held those papers, I felt calm and safe. Even when they started shouting and yelling and making us run through the gates into the camp, I walked on in a dream of serenity. I was going to be all right. I was going to survive. I can't explain it. One guard lashed me with a whip for being too slow, and I just turned and looked him in the eye. I couldn't believe it, but he backed off like he was terrified of me. Perhaps I was bathed in Jehovah's light? Who knows?

'The other Jehovah's Witnesses in the camp found me strange, I suspect, but I just did what they did and learnt as much as I could about their religion. Overhearing two guards talking gave me the best insight into their reputation. I had to be completely honest and never steal anything, not even the food we were all so desperate for.

'That wasn't an issue in the camp because there wasn't any, but once I was moved to the Hoffman's house as a nanny, it was incredibly hard. I'd learnt to grab every opportunity with both hands while I was in the ghetto and then on the run, so it took every grain of self-control to ignore food lying around in their house.

'The evil glint in Magda's eyes gave me strength. She was testing me, trying to trap me, and I would not give her that satisfaction. She even tried to use the children to catch me out. "Offer Wanda some cake." It was safer to decline. "No, thank you, that is your cake, and you must eat it." After all, I was luckier than the women in the camp. There was none of that disgusting water they dared to call soup. My rations were tiny, much smaller portions than the children ate, but there was nourishment in it.

'And although I had to sleep on the floor in one of the children's rooms, it was warmer and quieter there than in the barracks. And they deloused me before I set foot in the house. I could only wash in cold water, but at least it never froze like it did in the camp. No, I never forgot how lucky I was.

'I also had the consolation of the youngest children. They weren't old enough to pick up on the menacing atmosphere in the house. To them, I was just Wanda, a provider of comfort and fairy tales and lullabies. I was wary of the older children; they'd obviously been told I was a dangerous criminal, and they were allowed, even encouraged, to boss me around.

'I remember your wife and children coming to visit. It was the first time in many months that an adult had looked at me with sympathy in their eyes, with kindness. I can't tell you how much that buoyed me up. It was the same when we arrived at the farm. She was kind; she whispered to me "You're safe now." I wasn't certain what she meant. I had my hopes, but I'd learnt not to have any expectations. When she said I wasn't going anywhere, I didn't know whether to weep with joy or scream with laughter at the furious expression on Magda's face. In the end, I did what I always did and hid my emotions, looked down at the floor and waited. When you both left, I collapsed in a heap.

'She has been beyond wonderful to me. All the care she's given me, the clothes she's shared, the planning she's put into feeding me without upsetting my digestive system. When you've been starved for so long, it takes a long time to get over it. She was the one who told me to chew my food slowly and it really helped.

'Then there's the status she's given me in the family and in front of the children. I had to ask her to let them leave the table when they'd finished eating. "But it's a matter of respect, Wanda," she said. Respect for someone who was a criminal only a few weeks earlier. You've no idea how special that made me feel, how healed.'

'Henni is a wonderful woman, I agree.'

'That's why I had to be harsh with you the other day. She needed you even if she couldn't articulate that need and I was damned if you were going to indulge yourself instead of going to her.'

'No, I know. I hated you for saying it, but I knew you were right.'

Lottie stirred, grumbled, and then shouted. 'I can't move my arms. I can't move my arms. Help, help. My head, my head.'

'I'll fetch Henni.'

Heinz knelt by her chair and spoke words of comfort in a low, mellifluous tone. Henni came running out, wiping her hands on her apron.

'What is it, Mama? What's happened?'

'Help me, help me.'

'She said she can't move her arms and something about her head.'

Henni massaged her arms and lifted first one and then the other. Her mother looked on as if watching a miracle, her eyes widening and her mouth dropping open. Her wrinkled face coruscated into a wide grin as she waved her arms around, hitting Henni in the face and throwing her off balance.

'Ow, careful. How's your head, Mama? Does it ache?'

'My head?' She seemed puzzled as she moved her head around, studied a cloud overhead and belched.

'I'm hungry. When are we going to eat?'

'Soon, Mama. Let's go inside now.'

Back at the seedbed, they pondered the interruption.

'I wonder what that was all about,' said Wanda.

'Who can tell? She may have been dreaming about something, or perhaps she was reliving her fall the other day. Or maybe it was something different. Henni said the doctor who diagnosed her condition wanted her to see a specialist in Munich, but we couldn't even find out if the man is still alive. Besides, we don't have enough fuel to get her there or enough money to pay for a consultation.'

'Would it do any good? I mean the condition is irreversible. She'll have periods of normal thoughts and behaviour but continue to deteriorate until she dies.'

'No, you're right. I suppose Henni and Gunter want to feel that they've done everything within their power to help.'

'They already have. They love her. You all do, I think. There's no greater treatment than that.'

'No, you're right. Tell me something, Wanda. Incidentally, what is your actual name?'

'Yehudit. It means praise in Hebrew.'

'That's rather beautiful.'

'You think? I've got used to Wanda. I owe her my life, after all.'

'I wanted to know how you knew. Did Henni tell you?'

'About the rape? Yes, she told me eventually, although by then I'd guessed.'

'How?'

'The bond of love between you is strong, I think. Your romantic, fairy tale beginning is a cliché, but the rise of Hitler soon put you under pressure. The way you handled it and supported each other and the way the death of your daughter brought you together rather than split you apart all resonated with me.'

'She told you all about that?'

'Yes, in snatches. Always there was a warmth to her words, a solidity to the picture she painted. You were her rock and she yours.'

Heinz nodded in agreement.

'So, it puzzled me to see you together – or rather not together – when you came back from the dead, so to speak. I could see that you were keen to re-establish your relationship, but Henni was reluctant. A peck on the cheek, a hand on her shoulder, and she froze. That had to mean a physical betrayal. You don't seem the type to gallivant around so that suggested a physical trauma happening to Henni. Rape was the obvious answer.'

'What a fool I've been. I should have picked up on those same clues. I should have been able to work it out for myself.'

'Don't be too hard on yourself. You probably would have done if you weren't emotionally involved. Henni is your wife, not a police case. Besides, there are other complications.'

'Like what?'

'What the war means to her.'

'I don't understand.'

'She'll tell you better than I can.'

Was Wanda right that he shouldn't be too hard on himself? He was disappointed, let down by his intuition. Was it pride coming before a fall? Had he become too involved in his own emotions to see what others saw clearly? He'd behaved insensitively, and that wasn't like him; at least he didn't think so. They needed to talk again; that much was clear.

CHAPTER 14

'But, Papa, you said we'd play cards again. You promised.'

'And we will.'

'You said that yesterday and the day before and the day before that.'

'Monika, stop. You know how difficult things have been with Oma.'

'Yes, but we can play when Oma has gone to bed like we did last time. I asked Wanda, and she said she wants to play, so it's not just me.'

'Well, we'll see. Maybe we can play tonight after supper if there aren't any upsets.' Triumphant, Monika skipped off.

'Don't go boasting to the others,' he called out.

Something niggled at his brain as he tightened a loose bolt on the tractor. His brain was all over the place these days; he couldn't imagine handling a police case; wasn't sure he was capable of the most basic rookie surveillance, let alone writing a report afterwards. That was it. Oh God, how could he have forgotten? How many days was it since he'd told Alp he would leave food and water in the den? What if somebody had already used it and found it wanting? He hadn't replaced the beers; he hadn't dug up the tin container; he hadn't provided a blanket. Alp would not be pleased.

Oily fingers wiped clean, he headed for the kitchen. He could hear Henni upstairs talking to Lottie. He grabbed some cheese, filled a bottle with water, and sprinted to the den. Somebody had been there: the container had been dug up and emptied of its sausage; the perimeter had been dug up in search of water or beer. The two empty bottles lay on their sides, accusing him of neglect. He cleared up, stamping down the soil, putting the cheese and water away.

Guilt slowed his return to the farm; he needed to make amends, but how without starting a potential row with Henni? The blanket would have to wait, but he could at least provide some more beer without arousing her suspicions. When he returned to the den, Alp was waiting for him.

Heinz braced himself for a rebuke, but Alp had either decided to say nothing or didn't know about the lack of provisions.

'The first railroader is on his way to freedom.'

'Good. Anyone I know?'

'Maybe. Maybe not. It's best not to ask and even better not to know.'

'As you wish. How are things on the outside?'

'That's a strange expression to use. Do you think of yourself as being in prison?'

'In a way. I'm used to living in cities. Nothing happens here. It's very restful and perfect for holidays, but I miss the buzz of being in the centre of things, of knowing what's going on, of participating. Do you know what I mean?'

'Yes, although you'd feel far more imprisoned answering to our oppressors on a daily basis. That's if you're lucky enough to avoid one of their camps where you really would be in prison. I tell you, Heinz, these Americans haven't got a clue how to run things. The entire country is a disaster area. The trouble is they need us, but they don't want us. Now their latest wheeze is this.'

Alp handed him several sheets of paper. When he unfolded them, he saw the title Fragebogen in German underneath words he worked out to mean Military Government of Germany. He skimmed through the questionnaire and handed it back.

'You have to fill it in if you're to have any chance of a job. Its sole purpose is to weed out any Nazis, which is a joke because they're exactly the people with the experience to help them out of this mess. I mean, look at this, forty questions just about the different organisations you were a member of ranging from the SS to the American Institute. Or this, how much money you earned in your various jobs. How are we supposed to remember details like that when they've bombed our homes and filing cabinets to oblivion? How did you vote in November 1932 and then in March 1933? Did you appropriate any Jewish property?'

Alp's voice whined like a mosquito; Heinz suppressed a sudden urge to slap him dead.

'You're legally obliged to answer all 131 questions truthfully, otherwise, it's an offence against the military government of Germany and they can prosecute you. They've already caught a couple of people falsifying the questionnaire. Trouble is that some traitor gave them all the information they need to check the answers. It makes you despair; it really does.'

'Are you still pursuing your other activities?'

'Yes, but to tell you the truth, our hearts aren't in it any longer. We still assassinate the odd collaborator here and there; terminate any American foolish enough to be out on his own; cut off supply lines where we can. I've got some enthusiastic Werewolves who'll probably carry on doing that for the rest of their lives.'

'God, I hope not.' The heartfelt wish slipped out.

'You're a strange one, Heinz. I'm never quite sure what to make of you. One minute supporting the cause, the next muttering against it. Your record was impeccable, although I did wonder why you never made it higher than Inspector. Did you show the same ambivalence in your work?'

'I'm just a realist, Alp. The war has ended. We lost. It's not surprising the Allies are getting their pound of flesh. I accept that I'm isolated up here and don't see as much as you do, and I'm as keen as you are to see ordinary soldiers get away, but surely, we would achieve much more with – he was going to say collaboration and stopped himself – with an understanding of what needs to be achieved. You said yourself they need us. Perhaps they would want us if the Werewolves gave up harassing them?'

'I like you, Heinz. Heaven knows why, but I do, so I'll just put this conversation down to political naivety. You keep supplying the den with food and water and I'll try to educate you in the ways of the world.'

Heinz was on the cusp of being offended when he saw Alp wink at him.

'All right, Alp. Let's leave it at that.'

The accusation of naivety troubled him, however; it linked to feelings of letting himself down and being a lesser man. It was still rootling around his brain when they sat down to play cards that night.

'Oh, Heinz, what did you do that for?' Gunter groaned as Wanda picked up a large pile of cards.

'I couldn't help it. You're the one who dealt me these cards.' Heinz blustered and made an effort to concentrate, knowing full well he'd given the pile away needlessly.

'I think you'd play better with a small drink inside you. I'll get one while Wanda is sorting out her cards. Would you like one, Wanda? Henni?'

The women declined except Lottie, who insisted on a Schnapps possibly because nobody had offered her one.

'What do you think, Henni?'

'Never mind what she thinks. I'd like a Schnapps and that's what I'm going to have.'

Henni shrugged. 'I don't suppose it'll do any harm.'

Play continued, punctuated by a shout of 'Prost' every time Lottie took a sip. She was enjoying herself when she let rip a prolonged and noisy fart. There was a moment's horrified silence and then everybody burst out laughing; nobody could stop and when a feculent whiff reached their nostrils, it set them off again. Lottie giggled away, though whether she understood the reason for everyone's laughter was anyone's guess.

'Stop, stop, I can't take any more. It's making my

stomach ache.' Henni wiped the tears from her eyes. She looked ten years younger and with a sharp pang Heinz remembered the photo he'd left behind in Krakow. He'd taken it in the early days of their marriage, hiding behind a tree while she played with a neighbour's dog; he'd captured her essence, perhaps because she didn't know it was being taken, and displayed it on his desk at work. She'd never seen it preferring to display a studio shot of their wedding on their credenza at home. One day he'd tell her all about it and how much it meant to him.

The game proceeded in a new atmosphere of jollity and companionship. They talked about good times as they played their hands. Even Lottie contributed with sensible memories of Henni as a little girl and the first time Heinz had come to the farm. Heinz made them laugh, remembering how nervous he had been asking for her hand in marriage. Wanda turned out to be a talented mimic and amused them with tales of a stuttering suitor. Gunter's face radiated happiness, and Monika sat proud and tall, delighted to be included in this grown-up party.

When the men won the game, and the evening ended, nobody wanted to leave. Cards were put away with infinite care; chairs were replaced now here, now there, as if they couldn't remember where they belonged; the card table dismantled; trips to the toilet made. Reluctantly, having run out of excuses, everybody made their way upstairs.

That night, in bed, Henni spooned herself into his back. How he longed to respond, to take her in his arms, to make love to her. He knew, even if his body didn't, that it was too soon; that she wanted warmth and closeness rather than intimacy.

'She fancies you.'

'Who?'

'Who do you think? Wanda, of course.'

'Don't be ridiculous. She can't be over 30 if that. She's hardly going to fancy a man in his 50s.'

'Why not? You're a handsome man and since you've been working on the farm, you've toned up and lost weight. You look much younger.'

The compliment was increasing his arousal.

'It's you I love, Henni.'

'I love you too.'

And he had to be content with that, although his dreams that night suggested all manner of fulfilment which he tried hard to remember in the morning without success.

CHAPTER 15

AT THE BREAKFAST TABLE, Heinz avoided looking at Wanda. He was embarrassed, even if he didn't believe his wife's assertion. Anyway, he needed to talk to Henni and find out more about – how had Wanda put it? – how the war had affected her, something like that. After Henni had given the girls their chores for the day, he suggested they both did a stock take, including the second larder and the other hiding places around the farm.

'Yes, good idea. I'm sure I've stored some chestnuts somewhere. If we find them, I could make some flour. It would be nice to eat bread again.'

He didn't dare mention Alp and the food he needed for the shelter, but they worked well together, moving provisions around, taking notes of what was hidden where, and although they never found the chestnuts, they were pleased with what they had achieved.

'Henni, you said there was a lot more you wanted to talk to me about. Shall we take some time off today to do that?'

'Yes, that's a good idea. Let's go up to Lisle's grave when Lottie is having her afternoon nap.'

'Great. I'll take a trowel and other stuff to tidy up the grave while we're there.'

At first, they worked without speaking. The sun had clouded over; the air was still warm with just the suggestion of rain to come. Heinz weeded and trimmed the edges; Henni washed the headstone and levered off moss and lichen; their scratching and scraping accompanied by the sweetest trill of a nearby thrush.

'I hope she didn't suffer.' Henni's words were scarcely more than a whisper.

'Why would she? If I understood the doctor correctly, the heart just gave out. It would have been peaceful, most likely while she was asleep.'

'If that's what happened.'

'What do you mean?'

'I never told you the full story, did I? There was a nurse who was supposed to be looking after us. She was evil, Heinz. I shall never forget the look on her face when the doctor told me Lisle had died. It was triumphant and ugly as hell. There wasn't the slightest hint of compassion in her face, not in her eyes, not in her hard mouth, not in the tilt of her head. It was a distressing time, but that look sent me over the edge. I screamed and screamed. I guess I was hysterical, so they gave me something to knock me out. When I woke up, you were there at my side, and she was nowhere to be seen.'

'She sounds a nasty piece of work.'

'The thing is when I returned to have my stitches out, she was there assisting the doctor, a different doctor this time. When he finished and left the room, I confronted her about her attitude. Do you know what she said? "Germany doesn't need children like that." I was furious. I said Lisle was special and beautiful and loved by both of us as much as any of our other children.

'That's when she said she was *special* all right and there was only one thing to do with special people and that was to get rid of them the way Hitler had ordered. And then she drew her hand across her throat. I couldn't fathom what I was hearing or what I was seeing, so I pressed her again: "Is that what you did with Lisle? Murder her?" She didn't admit it, but then she didn't deny it either. She just repeated what the doctor had said about her heart condition. To this day, I don't know what the truth is.'

'I wish you'd told me, Henni. I could have had her investigated. The doctor too, arranged for a post-mortem, sorted it out once and for all.'

'It wouldn't have brought her back.'

'No, but maybe it would have given you peace of mind.'

'Only if you found out it wasn't true.'

He went to sit down, the ground shifting like quicksand. He'd gone back to work knowing nothing about this aspect of Henni's trauma. Was he at fault? Should he have known? Henni had never even hinted at murder. Sitting by Lisle's grave, he felt a creeping shame. Colleagues had sympathized over the death of his child, yet he had never mentioned her disability. A heart problem, he'd told them, nothing about an extra chromosome. Was he ashamed? Or did he want to avoid discussion of Hitler's euthanasia programme? What would he have done if one of them had said something crass like "Maybe it's for the best?" or "Better in her sleep than with a lethal injection"? With the war over, it was easy for him to say he would have investigated the medical staff, but on what grounds? It wasn't something his bosses would have sanctioned for an instance.

'Actually, I don't think it would make any difference to me now, even if you had investigated it and found out she died a natural death.'

'What do you mean?'

'I'm angry, Heinz, and it's the worst kind of anger because I'm angry with myself. I've spent the last few years sleepwalking. How did I not know the Nazis were killing disabled people? I must have known and just put it out of my mind. I'd see the newspaper headlines and refuse to read the stories. I didn't want to know; I didn't want it to upset me. Sometimes I comfort myself with the knowledge that there were plenty of disabled people around Berlin, war veterans with no arms or legs, or blind, so they weren't killing every disabled person. But it's just an excuse. They probably put war disability in a different category in their warped, demonic minds.

'I remember seeing posters of disabled people around the city, but they looked like freaks, not like genuine people with disabilities. It didn't feel like it had anything to do with me. I suppose they were picturing disabled people in the same way they pictured the Jews, making them out to be so monstrous, so grotesque, that we wouldn't mind what happened to them so long as they were out of our sight.

'Do you remember that film everyone was talking about: "I Accuse"? It was about a doctor killing his disabled wife. We never went to see it, but I always assumed it was about a mercy killing, putting somebody out of their misery out of kindness, out of love, not because Hitler demanded it. But it was all propaganda, wasn't it? You can just imagine them discussing it: let's start by talking about mercy killing and then move on to murder. We've been so stupid, all of us, so gullible. And…'

'Go on.'

Henni started to speak, then changed her mind.

'I never told you about my visit to Albrecht and Magda, did I? I can hardly bear to talk about it, even now. I remember asking you once, what had happened to my Jewish friend Mrs Rose. Do you remember? And you said you didn't know. Is that true?'

'Yes, it is. I don't know what happened to her, or any specific Jew, but I suppose they didn't stand much chance in Hitler's Germany.'

'You see, you're still doing it now, even after the war is over. "They didn't stand much chance in Hitler's Germany." That makes it sound as if there was some small chance. There was none. They were killing them, Heinz. Those are the words you were looking for. Killing them.'

Heinz shifted his position, his mind racing ahead, fearing where this conversation was heading. Pin pricks of sweat formed on his back.

'Were you told about the Final Solution?'

'Final solution? No, it's not a term I've heard before.'

Henni sighed with a tiny rasp in her throat. It sounded like the last breath of a dying marriage.

'Albrecht told me about it. It was their euphemism

for murdering the entire Jewish population, eradicating them from the face of the earth, so that nothing, literally nothing, would exist of a whole people, not their religion, not their art, not their culture, nothing.

'They put them in concentration camps, but I never bothered to question what it was like. How they were starving them, ill-treating them. And those were the ones that could work. They were gassing all the others. Men, women, and children were forced into shower rooms with poisonous gas released from the shower heads instead of water. Thousands upon thousands upon thousands. Do you know what they did to the bodies? They burnt them. Massive, industrial-scale crematoria burning night and day to get rid of every last trace of them.

'People like my little brother and Magda regarded that as amusing. An imaginative solution to a terrible problem facing Germany. I felt physically sick listening to them. But even there, sat opposite my brother, I didn't say anything. I didn't call him out. I let him think that it was all right to do things like that in my name. But it wasn't, was it?

'And now it's over. The Allies have stopped them in their tracks, and I should be relieved, but I'm not. I wasted all those years when it was possible to do something, anything to stop the madness, and now I can't live with myself. I can't stand who I am. But I don't have a choice with three children to bring up, Mama to look after, Papa to support.

'I wake up every morning with a fog in my brain that never goes away. It's like a presence, like something tangible. I wash dishes, make meals, darn socks, scrub floors, and try as best I can to get to the end of the day without losing my way in it.

'Sometimes I think the only thing I do right is give Wanda food and a warm bed, but even then, I remember all the thousands I didn't do that for. How can I live with that knowledge? How can I live at all?'

She was crying now, hands searching pockets frantically for a handkerchief. Heinz retrieved his own and handed it to her. He didn't know what to say, didn't trust himself to find the right words. Her face spoke of torment, of sleepless nights, of wasted opportunities, of endless regret. This wasn't about a single incident that could be put right. It was about everything. How could he put everything right?

'Was that why you were prepared to kill Albrecht?'

'Yes. I never quite worked out how I'd do it, but there was no doubt in my mind that I would. I couldn't bear the thought of his smug face sitting at the kitchen table, revelling in the misery people like him had caused. When I look back now, I can't believe how close we were when he was growing up. He came to me with everything: his enthusiasms, his plans, his problems, his joys, his disappointments. I wonder if I would have supported Hitler at all if it wasn't for Albrecht. He joined the Party as soon as he could and the way he talked about Hitler and his plans for Germany sounded so wonderful, so absolutely right. I must admit, after a while, when he became more involved in the Party, he did get a bit boring on the subject, but I never imagined he was wrong.

'And then you came along. I fell in love and put all thoughts of politics out of my head. Do you remember how we used to talk and talk? We never ran out of things to say. It was one of the things that attracted me to you, your ability to listen and to say the right thing at the right time. I never had a boyfriend like that before. If they talked about important things, rather than motorcycles or cars, then it was only about themselves and their plans and their ambitions. They always told me what they were going to do in the future, but never asked me what I wanted. I didn't count at all until I met you.'

Heinz was on a tightrope, icy winds swirling around him, the balancing pole dipping now this way, now that. Below him, destruction, and chaos. Ahead, the face of his wife whose pain he was impotent to relieve. He had to keep inching his way forward and hope for the best.

'Do you ever wonder what happened to Albrecht?' he asked.

'Sometimes. So long as he doesn't come back here, I don't care. It would be better for everyone if he'd met his end in Krakow defending his beloved Fuehrer.'

'Death would be better than being taken prisoner by the Red Army.'

'Huh, don't worry about that. A fanatic like that would have saved the final bullet for himself. And laughed as he shot himself. His very own final solution.'

'Oh, Henni, you sound so bitter.'

'I am bitter. How can I be anything else? I can't see my way out of this fog, and I can't change the past, which is what I want to do more than anything else.'

'The fog is the past. The more you want to change it, the thicker it becomes.'

She tilted her head to one side, eyebrows furrowed, as she examined the idea, moving it this way and that, turning it over in her mind like a curio.

'I'm not sure what you're saying?'

Heinz, edging his way along the tightrope, wasn't too sure what he meant either, but having caught her attention did his best to continue.

'The past has swamped you. You can't see your way out of it, so you think the solution is to change it even though that's not possible. But there is another way of looking at it: the past can inform your future. It can be the light that draws you forward and the push you need from behind. All the bad things that happened, all the good things that happened, they're all interconnected. Instead of seeing your memory as a prison, see it as an obligation to the future.'

Henni, hands clasped under her chin in an attitude of prayer, looked intently ahead. Had he said enough? Should he continue? Or wait for a response?

'How would that work in practice?'

'I'm not sure. It may be something you work out by trial and error. Only you can say what is right for you, what will make you feel at peace.'

'What about you? Can you live with yourself?'

'Does it sound callous if I say I can? We did our level best to survive the madness that engulfed our country. Don't forget I saw first-hand what happened to people who expressed any doubt about what was going on, let alone spoke out against it. And I did what I could, when I could, to help people.'

'Yes, I know.'

'It seemed to me then and seems to me now that my first duty was always to you and to our children. I could not, with a clear conscience, do or say anything that put my family in peril. If that makes me a bad person, then so be it.'

'No, I've never thought that.'

'I also believe you have been much too hard on yourself. You forget the sort of surveillance we were under, the dangers of saying the wrong thing or doing the wrong thing. My being in the Gestapo only afforded us a certain amount of protection. If, for example, they'd caught us harbouring a Jew, then they would have carted us off to one of those concentration camps and handed our children over to a childless Nazi family. How would you have coped with that?

'As an adult, I've never been interested in religion, but there's a phrase from the Bible that often came into my mind during these last few years. It's where Christ says you must hate your family to be his disciple, which rather contradicts everything he says about love, but I've always understood it to mean that it's better to be on your own if you want to follow your conscience.

'I'm not saying I would have been brave enough, but if I was going to speak out against Hitler, I needed to be a bachelor, not a family man. I love you, Henni, and I love our children and I would never do anything to endanger you or them. If I lost you or them because of something I'd said or done, that's when I wouldn't be able to live with myself. Does that make sense to you?'

She nodded, 'Well, you've certainly given me food for thought.'

'Have you spoken to Wanda about how you feel?'
'Yes.'
'And?'
'She has a very different take on it.'

The first drops of rain fell, and a brisk wind whistled through the trees.

'You should ask her. Now come on, quick, let's gather up the tools and go before we get soaked to the skin.'

CHAPTER 16

RAISED VOICES WOKE HIM. Another sensual dream interrupted, he threw off the bedclothes, grabbed a dressing gown and rushed downstairs pulling it on as he went.

'What's going on? You're going to wake the entire household.'

Monika, petulant and moody, stood with her arms akimbo. Heinz noticed soft mounds through her nightgown. She wasn't old enough to be developing breasts, surely? His cheeks burned as he wondered if he should even have noticed. Henni's face registered anger, dismay and concern in equal measures.

'Is somebody going to tell me what's going on?'

'Our daughter thinks it's acceptable to go snooping around, finding my private diary and then reading it cover to cover.'

'Oh, Monika, that's unworthy of you. How would you like it if someone read something private of yours?'

'What do you care? You don't trust me either. Neither of you do. How do you think that makes me feel? It's like I don't belong in this family and never have.'

Red-faced and sobbing, she ran out of the room and stormed up the stairs.

'Bloody hell, I wasn't expecting that for breakfast.'

'I'd better go up to her.'

'No, leave her, Henni. Tell me what's been going on and then we'll discuss the best way to handle it.'

'When we moved back to the farm when I was pregnant with Lisle, I started to keep a diary. Like all diaries, it was personal and revealed my feelings about many things including Monika's love for Hitler and our fears, my fears, that she might denounce us to the authorities if she suspected our stance on things.'

'Oh.'

'Yes, oh.'

'Would you mind if I read the diary?'

'No, of course not.'

'How did you find out she'd read it?'

'I went into her bedroom this morning to pick up her washing and found it wrapped up in one of her vests under the bed. It's almost as if she wanted me to find it. She's never been tidy, but she could have hidden it somewhere I wouldn't have dreamt of looking. I must have gasped out loud because she woke up and realised straightaway that I knew. I told her she'd better come downstairs, and that's when things became heated.'

'At least it's lanced the boil. The diary must be the reason for her scowling at you, although it could be her hormones as well.'

'Her hormones?'

'You haven't noticed?' Heinz made the shape of a mound on his chest.

'Oh, no, not that as well. I hoped she would be spared all that for a few more years.'

'It struck me as young.'

'It's hereditary, I think. I grew up faster than other girls in my class. We need to sort out this diary business before I tell her about the birds and the bees.'

'How long will it take me to read?'

'Not long. Look, I can't leave her up there feeling so upset. I need to go up and, at the very least, reassure her we love her as much as we ever did.'

'Yes, I don't disagree. Let me have the diary and I'll go upstairs and get dressed.'

Heinz focused on the diary. Henni's words catapulted him into Hitler's Berlin. A patchwork of images came to mind: lavish ceremonies and parades; Hitler in his Mercedes Tourer motionless in the foot well, right arm outstretched in salute; pristine buildings forming a dream-like world metropolis; the black-white-red banners and flags adorning rooftops and balconies; people of all ages cheering with loud hurrahs.

Beneath the pomp lay another city soon to be acclimatised to war: wooden barracks covered in roofing felt housed foreign workers; propaganda posters wall-papered every available space; cold, damp and malodorous cellars sheltered terrified civilians; a complex rationing system mocked the rainbow with seven colour-coded ration cards; balconies became home to rabbits for the pot. Then came the bombers night after night and destroyed both cities.

His fragmented memories unsettled him. It was so easy to be wise after the event, but he wondered now if they had been right to handle matters as they did. Early in their marriage, they had nearly rowed about politics when Henni had sided with her brother's fanatical views about Hitler and the Jews. As a result, Heinz proposed that they never discuss politics or religion or anything that might cause tension between them and Henni agreed. It was a pledge made of love, and when their world turned upside down, it seemed to serve them well.

It would be hard to explain to Monika now how an atmosphere of fear pervaded the entire city. They were sandwiched between the government at the top and the block wardens at the bottom. Even now he had to admit it was a clever set-up. The wardens were the first point of contact for people needing help from the state such as ration cards; they were also responsible for the political supervision of their allotted households. As the eyes and ears of the regime, they reported any suspicious conversations or behaviour to their Party superiors; they, in turn, passed them on to the Gestapo for further investigation.

It didn't matter that the Blockwarts were almost universally despised; the power they yielded added to the general sense of fear that you were always being watched. They had a particularly nasty 'stair terrier' at their first flat in Berlin; small in stature and as obsessed with Nazi ideology as a dog with a bone, he drove Henni mad with his constant demands and intrusions into their life. At that stage, Heinz was still a detective in the Kripo and had little to do with official snoopers.

When he joined the Party and moved across to the Gestapo, they were able to move to a larger apartment where the block warden was careful not to offend Henni for fear of what Heinz might do. He wasn't proud of his behaviour towards the ex-boxer. He was always polite, but he would hang around a fraction too long in his company, nodding his head and narrowing his eyes as if remembering some repugnant bit of gossip from his files. It was a pantomime performance, but like most of these petty officials, the warden wasn't bright, and his bullying tendencies could be cowed by an authority figure standing up to him.

Inside their apartment, which they feared might be bugged, they made sure their conversations were innocent, maybe even boring. They developed a code to use indoors. When Henni visited her Jewish friend, Mrs Rose, she would say "I had coffee and cake today." When she wanted to complain about shortages in the shops, she would say, "I didn't fancy buying any meat or toilet paper or sugar or whatever today. I'll get some another time." They listened to music on their gramophone and played card games. When the children arrived, they both loved being parents and found it easy to ignore the outside world as they delighted in first steps taken, first words spoken.

Occasionally, he wondered what their conversations would be like if they were able to talk as freely as husbands and wives should and as he remembered his parents doing all the time as he was growing up. He guessed Henni had changed a great deal since moving to Berlin; knowing how dangerous their world had become and how insidious the surveillance was, he was glad that their communication was limited to random sentences on their regular walks and freer conversations in isolated areas of the local park.

Suspicion and accusation could come at you from anywhere, as Heinz discovered in the Gestapo. Berliners seemed to fall over themselves in their rush to denounce neighbours, former friends, and even members of their own families. To complain about any aspect of life under the Fuehrer could find you interrogated. Silly things like adding a bit of graffiti to a poster or singing a ribald song were enough and malicious accusations abounded as people stuck the knife in business rivals, adulterous partners, and more prosperous siblings.

Henni never complained about her life. It was only now that he wondered if she had been lonely. His parents entertained frequently, and the house was filled with the sound of conversation and laughter, music, and the chink of glasses raised in toasts. Mrs Rose had been a good friend to Henni but then disappeared along with the rest of Berlin's Jews. "I miss my coffee and cake." Had there been anyone else? He didn't think so. It was easier for him. Notwithstanding his distaste for some of the Gestapo's handiwork, he had an office to go to, colleagues to talk to, secretaries to make him coffee. Henni only had the children and the cleverest one was a Nazi in the making.

She had done a wonderful job of bringing them up in difficult circumstances. He'd always known that; perhaps he should have done more to voice it. With his arrival at the farm, he should have taken on more responsibilities regarding the children instead of worrying about his own survival. Guilt thickened his throat; he pulled at his shirt collar, easing his neck upwards. In particular, they – no, he – should have taken the time to sit down with Monika and explain why they were all so pleased to hear the news of Hitler's death.

The children had already gone to bed when Gunter switched on the radio. "Achtung!" followed by a drum roll was the first thing they heard; they all looked at each other, not daring to speak. Wagner's music filled the kitchen. Twilight of the Gods. It seemed appropriate. Another announcement followed: "Achtung! Achtung! The German broadcasting system is going to give an important German Government announcement for the German people."

More music followed. This time Heinz recognized the dramatic strains from Das Rheingold. Gunter pointed out the significance of a German Government announcement when they were all used to hearing statements by the Fuehrer. Could this be it? They hardly dared hope.

The slow movement of Bruckner's 7th Symphony followed. Then the music stopped. There were three rolls of the drums, a moment's silence, and then the news of Adolf Hitler's death. At first, nobody uttered a word, and then Lottie said, 'Is it over then?' though whether she meant the music, the broadcast, or the death of a tyrant, wasn't clear.

'Yes, Lottie, it is over.'

Henni was crying as she hugged her mother; Lottie absent-mindedly patted her daughter's shoulder; Gunter poured out drinks for all of them and they toasted a future without Hitler.

'They'll surrender now, surely?' said Gunter.

'Please God they do,' said Henni. In the end, it took them another week.

Nobody found sleep easy that night: each of them remembering the effect of Hitler's rise to power on their lives. Heinz watched the bedroom turn from velvet black to blue-black to indigo-grey; the outline of the wardrobe and chest of drawers slowly becoming clearer. He must have fallen asleep, only coming to consciousness when the dawn chorus started. Listening to silvery crystal sounds, repetitive rattles, single notes, and descending songs filled his heart with optimism. Their world would recover; if the birds could still sing, then so could the German people.

He was sitting at the breakfast table when his children came racing downstairs, competing to be first. Their lively voices created a different chorus, every bit as beautiful to his ears, and he smiled broadly as the children kissed him good morning. Monika was quick to notice that something had changed.

'What's happened?'

'Why?'

'You're all different. You're all smiling. Did we miss something?'

'Yes, you're right, Monika. We're smiling because Hitler is dead. The war is finally coming to an end.'

'The Fuehrer?' She flinched and turned away. When she spoke again, her voice was shaky.

'Why? How? I don't believe it.'

Oblivious to her distress, Heinz had prattled on about the radio announcement, the lack of any details, their hopes of a quick surrender and the return to normal life. He berated himself now for his lack of sensitivity. He seemed to be doing that a lot these days.

He flipped the diary pages back to the early entries, releasing a chocolatey aroma. Henni's childish scrawl revealed a little girl's small world: "Got up. Went to school. Played with Birgit at her house. Had noodles with cheese for supper. YUMMY." He couldn't blame Monika for wanting to read about her mother's early life; she wasn't to know the tempestuous information that followed just a few pages later. He started to plan his conversation with Monika. The diary praised how clever she was, which would have pleased her and could prove useful. It should be possible to explain things to her, shouldn't it?

The most damaging section was Henni's reference to schoolchildren denouncing their parents and her fear of Monika doing just that. That was linked to her recurring nightmare featuring Monika's teddy bear as a huge and threatening Nazi with swastikas for eyes. He remembered colleagues at work talking about their strange dreams, without ever going into details, and when he could recall his own night-time experiences, they were claustrophobic, frightening, and bizarre. Unnerving dreams seemed to be a widespread phenomenon in Hitler's Germany.

* * *

'I wish you had known my parents.' They were walking up to Lisle's grave at Monika's request.

'You never talk about them.'

'No, I suppose I don't. Their deaths came at the worst possible time for me. The Great War had ended with the loss of so many lives. Mine could so easily have been one of them. I was looking forward to spending time with them. I was looking forward to peace and quiet, to the love and care that only parents can give you.

'There are people who seem to find their inner selves in war. The "kill or be killed" atmosphere that pervades the training ground seems to awaken something inside them. They achieve their potential. They flourish on the battlefield. I wasn't one of them. As the years dragged on, I felt I was losing some connection with myself. I was becoming an automaton with a gun rather than a human being. Can you understand that?'

'I think so.'

'I watched as other men talked of their families and re-read their letters from home endlessly. All I could do was clean my gun diligently, and all I wanted to do was sleep whenever I had the chance. I was desperate for the war to end and then desperate to get home. But all I had was the briefest of reunions with my parents and then they both succumbed to the Spanish flu.'

'What was that?'

'Do you know what a pandemic is? It's a disease which spreads over a very large area and infects millions of people. So, the Spanish flu was a particularly nasty flu that spread all over the world and killed many people including your grandparents.

'I was devastated, not just because they died, but because I thought maybe I had been the one to infect them. The doctor didn't think that was likely because I never came down with the flu myself, but I always had a niggling little doubt.'

'Does flu always kill you?'

'No, not at all, unless you're very old or very ill already. You don't have to worry about catching flu now. This was just an unusual and deadly variety. We haven't seen anything like it since.'

'But it could come back?'

'I guess so, but it's not likely. This was years ago, long before you were born.'

'What were they like?'

'My mother was a beautiful woman. She was taller than my father, with long hair she could sit on. She had smiling eyes and a beautiful voice. She used to sing, and my father would accompany her on the piano.

'Papa was an accountant, and don't ask me to explain what that is, because I never really understood. He had to prepare and examine financial records and make sure they were accurate, but apart from being good with figures, I have no idea what the job entails. I'm sure he was good at his job, but he never seemed particularly keen to go to work and was always delighted to get back home again, so I'm not sure how much he enjoyed it.

'They loved each other very much and were happiest when they were together. They only ever argued about one thing. When my father had somebody new come to work for him, either a maid at home, or a new employee at his office, he would leave a small sum of money lying around.'

'Why?'

'To test the new employee and see if they were honest. It used to make Mama angry. She said it was wrong to do that, that it wasn't a test, it was a trap, and you should never put temptation in someone's way.'

'I think she was right.'

'Yes, I do too.'

The headstone glistened in the morning light. Monika ran her fingers over the inscription; when she turned to Heinz her voice was tremulous.

'Do you think they killed her?'

'I'm not sure, Monika. The sad thing is that it's entirely possible. Hitler thought disabled people had no right to exist. He thought a lot of people didn't have the right to exist, so he had them killed. People like Wanda.

'Why Wanda? She's not disabled.'

'No, but she is Jewish.'

'Jewish? But she doesn't look anything like... oh.'

'You were going to say she doesn't look anything like the Jews in your school books, weren't you?'

Monika nodded.

'If I wanted you to hate dogs, I wouldn't show you pictures of cute little puppies or attractive adult dogs with appealing eyes and cuddly fur. I would show you pictures of nasty-tempered snarling dogs with big teeth dripping blood. That's what Hitler did with the Jews. He hated them and wanted everyone else to hate them too.'

'So, he made them look horrid.'

'Exactly.'

'The diary said that a Jewish soldier saved your life during the Great War.'

'That's right. A man called Isaac Bernstein. He was

awarded the Iron Cross for his bravery, but that didn't make any difference to Hitler. He was Jewish, so he had to go.'

'Go where?'

'Those that could, left the country; those that couldn't, were killed.'

'That's awful, Papa. I'm so sorry.'

Heinz hugged his daughter close, whispering that none of it was her fault.

'When Hitler came to power, he wanted everybody to behave a certain way and think a certain way. He didn't want any discussion or disagreements. Anybody who spoke up against him or what he was doing ended up in prison, or worse. People quickly became frightened of saying the wrong thing or doing the wrong thing.

'Do you know what brainwashing means? Well, imagine someone taking your brain where you have thoughts and opinions and things you like and don't like and things you want to say and do, and that someone starts scrubbing it with soap and a brush. Suddenly you don't have any of your own thoughts and opinions; they've all been washed out of your head. Then Hitler comes along and puts all his own thoughts and opinions in your head instead.

'That's what happened when you attended school. Your teachers were all specially chosen by Hitler to put his thoughts and opinions in your head. That's why you wanted to start the day the German way with Heil Hitler; that's why you wanted to have a portrait of Hitler in the apartment; that's why you wanted to join the League of Young Girls. You wanted to please your teachers and to fit in with your classmates. But they also told you that it was your duty to report anyone who didn't support Hitler with their heart and soul. Didn't they?'

He waited and slowly Monika nodded her head.

'We love you, Monika, and we know you love us and wouldn't want anything bad to happen to us. But we also know, which you didn't at the time, that you had been brainwashed by your teachers.

'Now, imagine coming home from school and hearing us say bad things about Hitler or what he was doing. How would you cope with that? It wouldn't be fair to you. It would be like a test. Or a trap. It would be like leaving a small amount of money lying around.'

Monika's expression was pensive; her eyes dark as she stared ahead. When she spoke, her words were hesitant, subdued.

'It feels horrible. I feel horrible like my head is dirty or something. I don't think brainwashing is a good description. I think it should be called brain-dirtying.'

'It happened to many, many people. You've nothing to be ashamed of because it's easier to brainwash a child than a grown-up, but lots of grown-ups stopped thinking for themselves and accepted everything Hitler said.'

'But if it happened once, it could happen again. How can I be certain my thoughts are ever my own again?'

Momentarily stumped, he chuckled. 'Because, my lovely daughter, you are an extremely clever girl and now that you are aware of the dangers, you will always ask yourself questions whenever somebody tells you something or you read something. You will always weigh up the good things and the bad things about everything and then you will understand what is right. Only you can go through that process so you will know the conclusions are your own thoughts. Now come and give your old Papa a big hug and we'll head for home. And on the way, I'll tell you all about Isaac and his sisters and the life they led before Hitler came to power.'

CHAPTER 17

Lottie sat clutching a comb in her hand. She turned it this way and that. Mouth open, she let it drop into her lap. She started wriggling and turning her head away. A whimper escaped from her throat. Carola ran up and picked up the comb.

'It's all right, Oma, it's a comb. Look, you brush your hair with a comb.' She pulled it through her own hair. 'Do you want me to comb your hair?'

Lottie shook her head in fear, teary eyes looking for an escape route. Carola hid the comb behind her back and stroked Lottie's hand. 'It's all right, Oma, it's gone now. There's nothing to be afraid of.'

His stomach flipped over with pity; he shared an understanding smile with Carola. He was fortunate to have such exceptional children. Their life could have been so wonderful without Hitler and the war. It could still be satisfactory, he supposed, if Henni could come to terms with her conscience. He was eager to find out Wanda's views, but today the farm had to come first.

They were taking the sow to a neighbour's boar; it was one of the few occasions, outside the harvest period, when Gunter was prepared to use the tractor and trailer. A good litter would pay for the boar's services, provide a variety of meat and sausages for the family, and enable Gunter to exchange a piglet or two for fuel on the black market.

There had been daily inspections to ascertain when Else was ready to receive the boar; Gunter was so matter-of-fact with his explanations that nobody was embarrassed. Only Heinz was a little taken aback to discover the boar had a corkscrew-shaped penis. He had an image of a wine bottle being uncorked and a pig twirling round and round.

'Why don't we have our own boar?' said Tomas.

'Boars can be difficult to handle, and they have enormous appetites. If you've only got one sow like we have, it's not worth the bother. Joachim has around twenty sows, maybe more now, so it's worth it for him.'

Heinz carried the pail full of enticing kitchen scraps and sliced up apples and led Else up the ramp. All the children helped, holding boards to guide her on board, and now they wanted to see the other end of the operation.

Gunter drove down the lane with the children perched in the trailer with the pig, scratching her nose and back while she grunted with pleasure. It was a slow journey and Heinz kept up with them with an easy stride. If his Kripo colleagues could see him now. A workaholic, he had to be forced to take annual leave and always headed for the mountains to reinvigorate himself. In those days, youth made up for his unfit body and he walked miles; then came marriage, the luxury of home-cooked meals, and the unwelcome appearance of middle-aged padding, like too much butter spread on a slice of bread.

Even when war broke out and food became scarce, it proved hard to shift the excess weight. When they acquired an allotment plot near their home in Berlin, Heinz dug over the ground; the effort sent his heart racing and made him worry about his health for the first time. He thought about consulting a doctor, but when the symptoms subsided, so did his fears, and he never did anything about it.

Henni asked him to build a fox-proof cage so they could keep hens. It was a solid construction, but he wondered if his fellow Berliners, rather than foxes, would prove to be a bigger problem. He needn't have worried: the canny allotment holders organized themselves and hired someone to act as a security guard. The man turned out to be a thug Heinz had once arrested for robbery; with his scarred face and broken nose he looked the part, and there were never any thefts. As well as his wages, they gave him any surplus vegetables to eat or sell. It was a good deal, and both sides were happy with the arrangement.

Tomas loved being at the allotment, far more than the girls. He never stopped still inside the apartment, but out in the fresh air he became a different child, almost studious in his approach to gardening. When he was older, Henni gave him a small section to grow whatever he wanted. She offered the girls their own sections too, but they were more interested in the chickens and collecting their eggs.

An elderly man in the next plot took a real shine to him and taught him the names of different plants and how to look after them and what he called "companion planting" putting the right vegetables next to each other or even vegetables and flowers side by side. He'd forgotten all about companion planting and wondered if Gunter believed in it. He would have to ask him. Lost in his memories, the journey soon passed, and before he knew it, they were at Joachim's farm. The children scrambled down from the trailer and waited while the men greeted each other and chatted for a while.

'Right. We'd better get going then,' said Joachim. 'If you reverse the tractor and trailer next to that pen, she can go straight in. The boar is just on the other side so they can get used to each other for a few minutes before I open the gate.'

Seconds later, the boar heaved himself up on the fence, threatening to demolish it in his eagerness to meet Else. Joachim chuckled to himself and opened the gate. Guttural noises filled the air as he smelt her rear end; Else assumed an air of nonchalance and started to root in the ground, but the boar was having none of it and nudged her once or twice to remind her there was business to be done. She stood stock still as the boar mounted her. Joachim checked that all was in order, and they all lounged around, watching with varying degrees of interest.

'Does he feel heavy on her back?' said Monika.

'Not really. She braces herself so it feels quite comfortable. It's like when you put a rucksack or a satchel on your back. If you stand with your feet apart and expect the weight, then it doesn't feel so bad, but if I just threw it onto your shoulders, your knees would buckle, and you'd most likely resent it.'

'Does she enjoy it?'

'Oh, yes, she thinks he's the most handsome prince in the world and she's the luckiest princess that ever lived.'

Heinz smiled and wondered if Henni had managed to have her sex talk with Monika. Perhaps she wouldn't need to after today; living on a farm made some things a lot easier to explain.

'Papa, can I walk back with you?'

'Of course, it'll be lovely to have your company.'

They set off ahead of the others. Monika slipped her hand in his; the gesture touched him, and he wondered how much longer she would want such closeness. He remembered one of his colleagues in the Kripo talking about his daughter growing up: one minute coming for cuddles and sitting on his knee, the next stand-offish and flouncing off to her room, never to return to their uncomplicated relationship. Her behaviour had hurt him and when the time came Heinz knew it would hurt him too.

'Papa, what did you do in the Gestapo?'

A fair question, although he wasn't sure how to answer it. To give himself time to prepare, he asked if she'd ever read "Emil and the Detectives."

'Oh, then I must ask around and see if anyone has a copy. I think you will enjoy it. It's set in Berlin and it's always nice to read about places you know. To tell you the truth, I was already a grown-up when I read it and I'm not ashamed to admit it. Anyway, I digress. I don't know when I first wanted to become a detective, but it was the only thing I ever wanted to do.

'Perhaps it was something to do with my father's test for new employees. Like you and like my mother, I thought it was wrong to do it, but it set me off thinking about what makes some people honest and others not. Why do some people commit crimes? How do we protect other people from those crimes?

'I'm not sure my parents were too pleased when I told them. They would have preferred me to choose something less dangerous like becoming a lawyer or a doctor. But the more they seemed to be against the idea, the more determined I became to do it. I started out as an ordinary uniformed policeman patrolling the streets of Berlin and then I trained at the Police Institute, which is famous the world over. I worked hard, got my college degree and was offered a place at the Institute's Officers School.

'That's when war broke out and put paid to my plans. It's very sad to think that I've lived through two world wars. Still, I suppose it's better than the alternative. Anyway, after my parents died, I reapplied to the Officers School and in due course joined the Criminal Police or Kripo as an assistant detective inspector. I loved being a detective. When I woke up in the morning, there was always a big smile on my face, and I hurried to get to work. I loved it so much I used to be one of the last to leave the office each night.

'Then Hitler came to power and changed the rules. Before that, no policeman could be a member of any political party, which I think is right. Policemen should be neutral in any situation. They are there to protect the public and catch criminals, not play politics.

'Suddenly, with Hitler in charge, there was tremendous pressure on people to join the National

Socialist Party, the Nazi Party. I resisted joining for as long as possible, but eventually I did. Then my boss at work said he thought I should move across to the Gestapo. It's difficult to explain but sometimes when your boss suggests something to you, he's not making a suggestion, he's telling you.'

'Like suggesting it's time for bed?'

'Yes, exactly. We make it sound like a suggestion, but you know, and we know that it's not something that's up for discussion. I didn't know what to do for the best. I was very conscious that I had a wife and family to look after and if joining the Party and the Gestapo helped me to protect them, then it seemed the right thing to do.

'Technically, my job in the Gestapo was to protect the state against its enemies. In itself, that isn't wrong. Countries, states, governments: they all have enemies who will do anything to destroy them. The problem arises when the state you are trying to protect turns out to be rotten.'

'When did you think the state was rotten?'

'Almost from the beginning.'

'Oh.'

'Mm, my telling you this doesn't put me in a good light, does it? I just hope you can try to understand what it was like. I felt sucked in like a piece of fluff in a whirlpool. I also saw with my own eyes what they did to people who criticised Hitler or his policies. Ordinary people were beaten up, sent to prison or concentration camps. If they did that to ordinary people, imagine what they would do to people like me within the Party. We were all caught in our own whirlpools. It was a time of madness.'

'Mama said you tried to help people?'

'I did. It doesn't seem much now or rather it doesn't seem enough, but, yes, I did what I could to help people. Instead of arresting someone, I would give them a stern warning. I would let people who were hiding from us escape. The trouble is I couldn't do it all the time, otherwise my bosses would suspect something and investigate me. I had to pretend to be loyal to the Party and to Hitler at all times. Everybody did.'

'Even Oma and Opa?'

'Yes, even them. Do you remember when you first came here there was a Nazi flag hanging outside the gateway? That was one small part of the pretence. And if you'd grown up here, you would never have heard either of them say a careless word against Hitler.'

'If you could go back in time, would you do things differently?'

'Ah, now you're talking about the wisdom of hindsight, where you understand things now that you didn't understand at the time. Yes, I would definitely do things differently.'

'What would you do?'

'Take your mother on honeymoon to Switzerland and ask for political asylum; that's where you ask to become a citizen of another country for political reasons.

Her mouth fell. 'Switzerland? I would have grown up like Heidi.' She attempted a little yodel.

'The trouble with re-inventing your past is that we can't be sure you would have been born at all. We might have had three boys instead.'

Monika gasped. 'Let's not re-invent the past then.'

'Don't worry. I wouldn't want to change you for the world and if that means I have to live with my past, then so be it.'

CHAPTER 18

IN BED THAT NIGHT, he told Henni about his conversation with Monika.

'Did she understand the pressures we were all under?'

'Hard to tell. I'm not sure we understand them. At least she knows I tried to do some good.'

'Unlike her mother.'

'Oh, Henni, come on, my love. Stop beating yourself up about something you had no control over. I had opportunities to help people, and I didn't always take them. I judged the situations as best as I could. That means people I could have helped suffered. Don't you imagine that plays on my conscience now?

'I had to avoid helping too many people in order to keep my bosses happy. How were you supposed to help people without drawing attention to yourself and endangering our children? You know what Hitler's views on women were. You had to stay in the kitchen, look after the children and go to church.

'Women were reported to the Gestapo for wearing make-up because that made them suspect in Nazi eyes. How on earth do you think you would have survived if you'd turned up at a concentration camp with food and clothing for the prisoners? Believe me, they would have found you a place inside sooner than applaud your Christian conscience.'

He hesitated for a moment, then spoke despite himself.

'And isn't there the tiniest bit of pride in all this?'

'What do you mean?'

'Well, wouldn't you like to pat yourself on the back and say, "I wasn't like the others."?'

'But I was. That's the problem.'

'But now you're wearing sackcloth and ashes like it's a badge of honour. The fact is, we all made a mess of things, and we need to admit it and move on. If we don't move on, we're letting them win.'

'Sounds like you've talked to Wanda.'

'No, I haven't had a chance to. Anyway, let's change the subject because this isn't doing either of us any good.'

He reached for her hand; she gave it a squeeze and turned on her side. He sighed and felt himself falling to the ground from a tightrope spread across the sky. Henni tossed and turned at his side. Had he spoken too harshly? He seemed condemned to taking one step forward and two steps back. Would there never come a time when they could lead a normal life and be a normal couple?

He heard a commotion coming from Gunter's room. It was probably Lottie deciding it was the morning and time to rise and shine. He considered getting up to help, but his limbs protested. Hadn't they walked a long way today? Weren't they entitled to some peace? Besides, Henni wasn't sleeping either; it was her mother after all; she could go. His eyelids were like pebbles weighing him down. Revisiting the past seemed to take more energy than digging over the garden. And then he was cleaning his gun, seated with his back against a trench wall and falling, falling into a deep sleep.

* * *

He overslept and was late for breakfast. Henni's face was taut; was she angry with him? Should he make some conciliatory gesture? He was still so tired. The effort of trying to make peace overwhelmed him. Lottie sat hunched at the table, pulling down her dress again and again; she didn't respond to his "Good morning" and muttered something incomprehensible.

'Is Lottie all right this morning?'

'She had an accident last night. It's probably playing on her mind.'

'An accident?'

'She wet the bed.'

'Oh, dear.' He stared at his empty plate. A one-off or a new level of complication in their lives? No wonder Henni's face looked strained. Anybody could deal with a single accident; the prospect of it becoming a daily occurrence must be whirling around her mind.

'I'm sorry. I should have helped you last night.'

Silence solidified the air between them; he guessed that meant she agreed with him.

'What will you do?'

'There's nothing I can do. We'll have to wait and see if it happens again. If it does, I'll have to investigate some form of nappies.'

'Is the mattress dry? Do you need me to air it for you?'

'No, her nightgown absorbed most of it, and the rest went on the sheet. I'll put an extra blanket on the mattress tonight.'

'Well, tell me if there is anything I can do.' He poured himself a cup of coffee and went outside. Carola was bringing in a basket of eggs from the henhouse; Monika was manoeuvring a wheelbarrow past the kitchen garden; no need to ask where Tomas was.

He had a list of odd jobs to do around the farm and didn't want to do any of them. He needed to check provisions in the den, but even that simple task seemed like a burden. Only the thought of seeing Alp and sharing news of the outside world propelled him through the forest.

He opened the container; the cheese was still there, maturing; it added a pungent smell to the herby surroundings of moss and earth. He sat down and closed his eyes. Perhaps a brief nap would restore his vitality? He considered his conversation with Monika. He'd been a boy of around 10 years of age when he'd visited Zurich with his parents. Was it a business trip for his father? He couldn't remember now or how long they stayed there, but he remembered his mother's delight at the range of shops and his own delight at the wonderful views. Was that where he formed his desire to visit the mountains of the world and hike through their lofty realms?

The idea of seeking political asylum in Switzerland had appealed to him over the years, but not when Hitler first came to power. He never imagined how bad everyday life would become. Besides, who was to say that Henni would have agreed to it? To leave behind your family, your country, was a big step to take and Henni had fallen pregnant early in their marriage, making a move abroad even less welcome. Still, Switzerland remained a beautiful country.

His breathing eased into a gentle snore, and he wandered narrow pathways surrounded by lush green open spaces with snow-capped mountains in the distance. Henni walked ahead of him holding Tomas by the hand; the girls gambolled around the Alpine meadows picking wildflowers and calling out to each other, louder and louder. Monika turned to him, dressed in the colourful clothes Heidi wore on the front cover of Henni's childhood book. She was yodelling and spinning towards him with a Nazi salute.

'Heil Hitler.'

Heinz shook himself awake. A thickset man with bushy eyebrows gawped at him and then jabbed his finger at him.

'Who are you?' Aggression masked fear.

'The same question was going through my head.'

'Are you Alp?'

'No, Alp isn't here. I've come to check the supplies. There's cheese and water. Not much, but times are difficult.'

'No matter. Pass them over. I thought you might be the guide for the next part of the journey. Bit early for that, I guess.'

'So, what's your story?'

'No stories. Not until we're free.'

'But Wehrmacht?'

'Wehrmacht? What gave you that idea? No, no, no. SS always and forever.'

'What the hell.' Heinz felt his cheeks burn and he cursed under his breath. 'I need to get back before I'm missed.'

'Cheers.' Water bottle raised in salute; cheese devoured.

Heinz headed straight for the house, whistled at the dogs, and picked up Gunter's tool set. He worked in a frenzy repairing the garden gate, replacing wooden slats in the hen house, re-attaching guttering on the lean-to.

'Don't stand still or you'll get nailed to the spot.'

'What?'

Blood was thumping in his ears; he turned away from Wanda; no need to take his anger out on her.

'What's happened? Why are you so angry?'

'I. Am. Not. Angry.' He drew in slow, steady breaths and gave her a false smile before going indoors.

'Suit yourself.' The words echoed around his brain. Henni was laying the table for lunch; he could smell something rich and gamey coming from a pot on the range; he made his excuses, grabbed some food, and headed out.

'I'm going for a walk. I won't be back for lunch. I need to clear my head.'

A fiery sun was beating down on him as he marched down the path towards the farm entrance; just before the turning, he set off across the scrub until he reached a forest glade. His head ached and his stomach growled. He sat down on a fallen log and bit off a chunk of cheese;

he hadn't realised how hungry he was. The creamy sensation on his tongue calmed him down.

Was he being stupid? Had Alp duped him? Had he lost his ability to rely on his instincts? The railroader's stolid appearance had awakened some deep distrust in him. They were looking after their own; they weren't bothered about their brothers-in-arms; they were out to save their own skins.

If anyone handled the worst excesses of Hitler's reign, it was the SS. Yet they were the ones making their escape from justice like rats leaving a sinking ship. He still hadn't told Henni about the use of the den. How the hell was he going to do so now? She would laugh at his naivety, mock him. He might as well tell her he was busy saving Albrecht's life; that really would go down well with her. Oh, God, what a mess it all was.

He clenched his jaw as tears formed in his eyes. Perhaps he should walk to the nearest Allied camp and turn himself in? Let them decide his fate. Or was that a coward's way out? Was he going to abandon his family because he didn't want to think anymore? Maybe he could tell the Allies about the den. Barter information for freedom? Would that work so that he needn't feel guilty about walking away? He finished the rest of the cheese. A soft breeze filtered through the trees and turned the glade into an oasis of reflective calm. He remembered how Isaac Bernstein had saved his life in No Man's Land. Who would save him now?

'Knock, knock.'

He turned his head. Wanda stood there, a yellow patterned dress contrasting with her dark hair and eyes. She looked stunning. For a moment, Heinz was speechless; he stared at her like a hungry dog.

'How did you find me?'

'It wasn't difficult. Anybody could see where you'd trampled through the undergrowth. I didn't know this was here, though. It's beautiful.'

'Do you want to sit down?' He moved along the log. He bit into an apple, still crisp and juicy, after months of storage. His mouth cleansed, he took another bite and offered her the apple. She took a bite, covering his hand with her own. A jolt ran through him. His heart seemed to shift inside his chest. "She fancies you" spun round his brain like a top. Warmth flooded through him; the hairs on his arm stood to attention while his whole body relaxed. He couldn't take his eyes off her. In all the turmoil of his mind, one action seemed obvious, necessary, uncomplicated.

'Do you want to tell me what's upset you?'

Right then, he didn't want to tell her anything, except how beautiful she was. All he wanted to do was run his hands over her body, fill her mouth with his tongue, fill her body with his own. His hand moved to stroke her hair. What the hell was he doing? And yet he couldn't stop. He took in every inch of her face: hazel eyes, now dark, now green; chestnut locks catching the sunlight in amber glints; lips moist and deep pink-red; the smell of apple as she breathed out.

His breath shortened as he caressed her breast; he shifted his position to ease the bulge in his trousers. She wasn't moving closer, but she wasn't moving away either. This was his responsibility alone; she wasn't going to make it any easier for him. And still, he couldn't stop, didn't want to stop, didn't understand why he was behaving like this.

'Oh, Wanda.'

Only then, with the heartfelt release of emotion in his voice, did she move forward, her fingers brushing his face, her lips pressing against his. Eyes wide open, they sank to the ground, kissing and caressing. They stopped, exchanged a questioning glance and then they were stripping off, lying naked and making love, oblivious to the world around them.

Sated, they lay gazing up into the sky.

'I cannot find the words to tell you how wonderful that was.'

'Yes, I know. I feel the same.' Wanda sat up, her face turned towards his, eyes smiling.

'But being practical, we had better get going before we're missed.'

While they were getting dressed, Wanda said, 'This may or may not happen again. Whether it does, or it doesn't, you will not at any time tell Henni.'

'No, of course not. What do you take me for?'

'I take you for a man. You do not love me. You love your wife. You love your children. One day, soon or in the years to come, you will feel guilty about what you have done here today and may do again. That does not give you the right to offload your guilt on Henni. What she does not know cannot harm her. Your confession, on the other hand, will destroy her. And don't change your behaviour either.'

'What do you mean?'

'Turn up at the farmhouse and start being super helpful or super attentive or super anything. Or start ignoring me. Or the reverse.'

'Oh, God, now I won't be able to move for fear of doing the wrong thing or saying the wrong thing.'

'Invoking God won't help, especially when you don't believe in Him.'

'Who says I don't believe in Him?'

'Henni told me. And yet you know your Bible. How is that?'

'My parents used to send me to Sunday school. The maid used to walk me there and take me to the park afterwards for an ice cream or a hot chocolate in winter. I enjoyed the stories and the woman running the classes was a kind soul. I was very fond of her.

'When I got older, I used to enjoy testing the boundaries, pointing out the contradictions, questioning everything. Bless her. I don't think she could cope with me, but she was always positive. "It's good to question, Heinz, because it strengthens your faith." She was wrong, but it took me a while to realise it. I kept going to church and then one day we were saying the Creed and I found myself embarrassed saying the words "God from God, Light from Light, True God from True God." It sounded like a load of magical incantations, hocus pocus, nonsense. And once I'd articulated that, I knew I didn't believe any of it.'

'Did your parents mind?'

'Not that I'm aware of. I don't remember telling them about my lack of faith. I said I would rather play with my friends than go to Sunday school and they agreed.

I wonder now if they were equally Godless and wanted me out of the house for some rumpy pumpy.'

Wanda laughed; it was a warm, full-throated sound. He smiled.

'Wanda, I wanted to talk to you. In fact, Henni suggested I did so. I wanted to find out how you coped with your experiences in the camp and during the war. There are also some things I'd like to discuss with you about our lives now, things I haven't told Henni about, well, not exactly anyway. Would that be all right with you?'

'Of course. Henni has promised to take the children on a picnic in the meadow. That would be a good time, unless you want to go too?'

'No, that sounds perfect. Thank you, Wanda.'

When she'd gone, he walked across the flattened grass and blushed. Just like animals leaving their mark. He headed for the stream that formed the southern boundary of the farm, stripped off and washed in the freezing cold water. At least he wouldn't return home smelling of sex, even if every nerve tingled with the memory of her body yielding to his.

CHAPTER 19

Heinz waved his family off and went looking for Wanda. He found her hanging out clothes on the washing line behind the farmhouse.

'Are you still happy to talk?'

'Yes.'

'And would you be happy to…'

'Have sex?'

'I've never met anyone as forthright as you.'

'Opportunities like this will be few and far between. Why waste time?'

'Where would you like to go?'

'Same place. Lottie won't manage to get far on this outing. Gunter will bring her back to the house soon. I don't want to be trapped in the bedroom with all its potential for turning into a farce.'

They made love with the intensity of new partners, both euphoric and anxious to please. She lay in his lap afterwards as he stroked and kissed her.

'Are you sure I don't love you?'

'Perfectly sure.'

'I'm not.'

'Don't be daft, Heinz. You're just a man with a healthy, sexual appetite. Nothing else.'

'You make it sound so romantic.'

'Enjoy it for what it is. Now, time to get dressed. I'll get the coffee on, and then we can talk. Find a different way back.'

As Wanda had predicted, Lottie and Gunter were in the house when he arrived back. Lottie was smiling and reminiscing about old times when Heinz walked in.

'Do you remember when we made love in the hayfield, Gunter?'

Heinz stumbled on his way to the sink. The shaving mirror reflected flushed cheeks and startled eyes. He washed his hands vigorously. He'd heard about blind people developing exceptional hearing; could people with dementia develop a sixth sense?

'We'd finished all the main stacks the day before and we were going back to cover them with canvas, only we became a little distracted.' She giggled and waved her dress about, revealing her pants.

'Lottie! Pull your dress down. That's not very ladylike.'

'I don't remember you complaining in the hayfield.'

Heinz dried his hands, turned, and winked at Gunter, who smirked. Just one of life's strange coincidences, he decided.

'Would you like me to look after Lottie?'

'No, you're fine. I find some of her memories quite enjoyable. I'll stop with her until the others get back.'

'Well, I'll take my coffee into the vegetable garden. See you both later.'

He sat on the garden bench until Wanda came out.

'We should do some weeding while we talk,' she

said, handing him a hoe. 'So, what's been bothering you?'

'I've been a fool.' He hid nothing as he told her about his meeting with Alp, the arrangements for the den, and his sudden realisation he had been duped.

'The trouble is, I can't pull out now. Alp isn't the sort of man you want as an enemy. He would be quite capable of revenge involving not just me, but everyone here. He has a streak of cruelty that I don't want to test.'

'Cruelty was a pre-requisite for SS membership.'

'Some would say the same for the Gestapo.'

'True.'

'I was never cruel, Wanda. I never tortured anyone. I want you to know that.'

'No, but your colleagues did.'

'I know and I don't know how they could do that. Anyway, what do you think I should do about Alp. Henni would go mad if she knew.'

'Don't tell her. Stick to the story you told Tomas. He told Henni the bad man didn't have a house anymore and was using the den as his home. She seemed to buy it.'

'Thank God for that. Still, it doesn't seem right to let it continue.'

'When a war comes to an end, people always hope there will be some great Day of Judgement: the good will be rewarded and the bad will be punished. It never happens that way. There'll be plenty of people, both good and bad, who won't get their just desserts. I imagine the worst offenders will get punished because of the enormity of their crimes, but not all of them.

The Allies will use those who are useful to them and conveniently forget their past misdemeanours. The vast majority of people will muddle along as best they can.'

'Do you think I've been a fool?'

'Naïve, perhaps, especially for an old soldier. When did army generals ever look after the foot soldiers first and save their own skins second?'

'The strange thing is, despite everything I've said, I quite like Alp.'

'You wouldn't if you had more choice. He's right about one thing: you are isolated up here. You have gone from being a man surrounded by colleagues, by subordinates, by superiors, to someone confined with his family. However much you love them, you're bound to find that oppressive. Alp offered you a taste of normality, a reminder of how you used to live. That's bound to be attractive to you.

'The reason Gunter remains so sane is that he has friends in the area, neighbours he's grown up with. He may not see them often, but it's enough to give him a sense of freedom. Apart from Alp, he's your only male friend. That must be hard on you.'

'Thank you.'

'What for?'

'Understanding the situation.'

'And the second thing?'

'Sorry?'

'You said there were a couple of things you wanted to discuss.'

'Oh, yes. Henni has talked to you about the war and her guilt about not doing more to help people oppressed by National Socialism. She told me you have a different take on the situation, and I wondered what that was.

'You seem, how can I put this without sounding rude, almost unscathed by your experiences? I guess that can't be true, but what's the secret to your moving on and my wife standing still or even going backwards?'

'I don't know, Heinz. My sympathy for Henni is boundless, not least because her kindness towards me was so important in those early days. Even when we weren't aware of what was going to happen regarding your return, I always felt safe. I understood Henni would never let me down. If Albrecht and Magda had turned up with a whole battalion of soldiers, she would never let me be taken away. We might all have died in the process, but not without a fight.

'I have told her many times how important she has been to me and to my recovery, but she needs to forgive herself, and that's something I can't do for her. Neither can you.'

'Would a pastor help?'

'If he were clever and sensitive. Anyone else might do more harm than good.'

'And is that what you have done? Forgiven people like Albrecht and Magda? Forgiven Hitler and all his henchmen?'

'I don't let their actions weigh on me. It's not a burden I choose to carry. They never sought my forgiveness, so the question is meaningless. If they wanted my forgiveness, they would need to repent of their actions, and I can't see that happening any time soon.

'Hitler is dead. Some of his henchmen are also dead. They cannot now seek the forgiveness of their victims. If you believe in God and in an afterlife, then you are content to leave such matters to Him.'

'Is that Wanda speaking or Yehudit?'

'Good question. Yehudit, I guess. I'm not competent to tell you in detail what Wanda would say about forgiveness. The Witnesses certainly believe in it, though. Don't misunderstand me, I believe in it too, but I see forgiveness as part of an ongoing relationship. That's why there has to be repentance so that my forgiveness is meaningful. Otherwise, it's just giving people carte blanche to do what they like.

'When I look at Henni, I see someone whose inability to forgive herself is a huge burden that weighs her down, that destroys her. Forgiveness is appropriate for her because she needs to mend the relationship with herself. She has, as far as I can see, never lost her faith in God, even if that faith isn't active right now. She needs to converse with God, acknowledging all the things she has done wrong and all the things she has failed to do, and then seek his forgiveness. If she does that in a sincere manner, then she will move on.'

'You said you don't let the actions of people like Albrecht weigh on you, that it's not a burden you choose to accept. So, if you can't forgive them because it's meaningless, are you choosing to forget what's happened to you?'

'I guess you could say so. But it's not forgetting in a mindless way, like Lottie forgetting things. It's saying I'm going to leave this to a higher court and, in the meantime,

I'm going to get on with my life unencumbered by the wrong done to me. I refuse to carry that as a burden for the rest of time.

'Does that make sense to you? I'm on a quite deliberate road to recovery. Active refusal of that burden is a conscious part of it. For the first time in years, I am doing exactly what I want to do, when I want to do it. Of course, there are limitations of circumstance. I can't eat a pork joint if there is no pig meat available. But, if it's there and I want to taste it, then I will do so regardless of the injunctions of the Torah.

'I find enormous solace in gardening. I never used to; now I can't get enough of the soil and the wonder of seeing seeds that I've planted unfurl and reach for the sun. When I first came here it was winter, so it's only now that I'm benefitting from the garden but goodness what a benefit! I would recommend gardening to everyone, including Henni. She used to be responsible for the kitchen garden. She needs to get back in charge of it.

'I'm still wary of meeting new people. That's why I was glad to hide when the American soldiers turned up. One day I will find out what happened to my family, but I suspect there will be no survivors. Perhaps that's why I'm wary. Just the thought of meeting new people reminds me of the people I've lost. That is why I am so glad to have all of you as my family. To rekindle normal relationships. And, yes, part of that has been initiating a sexual relationship with you.'

'Do you mean I'm part of your recovery programme?'

'Yes.'

'Bloody hell. You really are forthright. And yet, I can't feel offended. In a way, I feel privileged.'

'Good. That's a healthy response to a health-giving situation. The day will come when I need to move on. I don't want to leave any regrets behind.'

'I can't feel guilty about making love to you, Wanda. Maybe I should, but I can't. What about you? Do you ever feel guilty? Aren't you betraying your friendship with Henni?

She was silent for so long that Heinz wondered if he'd put paid to any further sex.

'It's complicated. We have lived through such appalling times and they're not back to normal yet and probably won't be for a very long time. I need this. I think you do too.'

Heinz nodded enthusiastically.

'In normal times, I wouldn't dream of becoming intimate with another woman's husband, friend or not. But I needed to know I could still function as a woman, and I wanted to do that with somebody who would be kind. I think at heart you're a good man. You could have backed Magda when we first arrived at the farm or forced me to go with her at the point of a gun, but you didn't. I think you were swept up in the Nazi storm like so many people were, but you tried to do some good while protecting your family. It doesn't exonerate you from being part of the regime, but it's a start.'

'Oh.' He looked down.

'Your estrangement from Henni shifted the ground from under your feet. It left you vulnerable, unsure of yourself, open to an approach from someone like Alp.

But you will go back to being a team again, I'm sure, a close and loving partnership, as before'.

'I hope so.'

'And perhaps having sex with me will help you be patient with Henni, will stop you feeling resentful and undermined. Technically, to answer your question, I suppose I am betraying my friendship with Henni, but emotionally I don't feel that at all. And providing she doesn't find out, no harm is done to her.'

'I still don't know what to do about Henni and her need to forgive herself, as you put it.'

'Leave it for the moment. I'll talk to her again when the chance arises. In the meantime, do all you can to help her with Lottie. Dementia is hard on everybody, but most of the care is still falling to Henni.'

CHAPTER 20

'Hurrah. Breadmaking begins again. The bees have been extra busy again so maybe even a cake. Now shoo, out of my kitchen, while I make the most of Mama's naptime.'

Henni was in a good mood: bartering with her neighbours had resulted in enough flour to last a few months; several weeks had passed without Lottie having another accident; the children were spending the weekend with Hans and Clara; the farm was as productive as ever.

Wanda had persuaded her to spend time in the kitchen garden on a daily basis and arranged what she described to Heinz as a "Ceremony of Forgiveness" with readings from the Psalms and the New Testament, both of them facing each other across Lisle's grave as a symbol for all the dead and all the victims of the regime.

Henni's progress didn't stop the lovers from indulging their passion. They were lying in the glade, wrapped in each other's arms. The sun warmed their bodies; they smelt of fresh air and sex. Around them, the sounds of the forest and the skies merged in a delightful concert of trills, chirps, twitters and whistles.

'I'm very grateful to you for helping Henni. She is a

different woman, almost happy. There are still moments when something like a shadow passes over her and she seems lost, but they are happening less often now.'

'That's good. Don't expect too much, too soon. Her journey will take time and go through ups and downs.'

'I know.'

They readied themselves to go back. Heinz headed for the stream while Wanda sauntered back. She was working in the garden when Heinz arrived, downcast, sitting in the front of an army jeep; the dogs were going berserk, pulling against their chains. Lost in his own thoughts, he didn't even bother to whistle them into silence.

Henni opened the door at the same time as Gunter appeared round the corner.

'What the hell?'

'Get those dogs under control or we'll shoot them.' The words came from the interpreter, though none of his companions looked bothered.

Gunter whistled, and the dogs went quiet. Henni came to stand beside him.

'Who is this man?' The interpreter jerked his head back at Heinz.

'He is my husband.'

'Who is she?'

'A friend.'

'It seems you have some explaining to do. We'll talk inside.'

He turned to the American soldiers, making suggestions in an undertone. The next minute, they were all seated around the kitchen table.

The Army captain placed his file on the table and spoke in a calm, measured voice.

'Tell them we're interested in the husband. Occupation during the war. Current situation, etc.'

Heinz gave the interpreter a potted history, ending with his faked death and current employment on the family farm. Nobody missed the soldiers' reaction when he used the word Gestapo.

'As you heard for yourselves, he's an Inspector of the Gestapo based in Berlin at the start of the war, then in Poland. Faked his own death to escape justice and basically a Nazi through and through.'

'Tell them we're taking him in for further questioning.'

'Excuse me, Gentlemen.' Wanda, cheeks flushed, radiated beauty. She spoke English with an accent that sounded very much like the captain's; the soldiers paid her respectful attention.

'I think, perhaps, your interpreter is following his own agenda here.'

Outraged, the interpreter tried to talk her down in German. She ignored him and addressed the captain.

'It is true that Heinz Bauer was an Inspector of the Gestapo. It is also true that he was a member of the Nazi party – a reluctant one.'

'When did he join?'

'1933'

'OK.'

'He faked his death, not to escape justice, but to cease being part of the Nazi machine of war. He hid on the farm because Nazi fanatics would have strung him up from the nearest tree as a deserter. He has nothing to fear from American justice.'

'How long have you been a friend of the family?'

'Since just before Christmas 1944.'

'How come?'

'I'm a former prisoner at Auschwitz, released to become a nanny to Obersturmbannfuehrer Hoffman of the Central Government in Krakow, a man I hope is dead or receiving suitable Allied justice. Hoffman is this man's son and her brother. He is also, in ideological terms, the black sheep of the family.'

'I see.'

'I hope you do, Captain. As I'm sure you realise, many people were swept up in the Nazi movement which made no allowance for dissent. Heinz was a career detective in the Criminal Police. When his boss suggested he joined the Gestapo, he had very little choice in the matter. However, he helped many people in that role. I don't know how easy it would be to find them, but they certainly exist.

'I, too, would be more than happy to vouch for this man and his family – except for the son. When Hoffman realised the war was ending, he arranged for Heinz to transport his wife and children to Bavaria. I came with them. From the moment I arrived at this farm, they gave me shelter and food and clothing. Quite simply, I was safe here.'

'A pleasant story, but not a likely one. How can we believe her?' Lips curled in a sneer, the interpreter pushed back his chair and strutted around the kitchen.

'What happened to Hoffman's wife and children?'

'The family refused to have them stay here, so Heinz drove them to the mother's village, Gerstenried, which is where, I presume, they still are. It was on his way back from there that he decided to fake his death.'

'Say, Cap'n, ain't Auschwitz where they tattooed all the prisoners?'

Wanda said nothing in response and placed her left arm on the table, turning it to reveal the blue-black numbers underneath. There was a sharp intake of breath.

'There's your answer, soldier.'

The door to the stairs creaked open and Lottie appeared, thumb in mouth, eyes staring. She ran to Henni and tried to get on her knee like a little girl.

'Lottie has dementia. You'll have to forgive her if she doesn't behave as you would expect a grown woman to.'

'No worries, Ma'am, she reminds me of my Granny back home.'

'Talking about home, something smells mighty good here.'

Everyone looked towards the range and Henni yelped. She checked the cake and brought it out to rest.

'Please don't take it from them. The children are staying with friends, but they seldom have sweet things to eat.'

'Why would we do that?'

'You did last time.'

The captain looked at the interpreter, who froze next to the cake he was smelling.

'Their larder's full and people are starving in the towns.'

'And these goods were booked into army stores, were they?'

'That I couldn't say.' He slid onto a chair on the far side of the room, ears turning bright red as the seconds passed, eyes studying the books shelved to his right.

Heinz wondered if his wife and father-in-law were feeling as he did: a theatre audience in a foreign land, or perhaps, more accurately in his case, prisoners in a foreign court. He grasped that Wanda was pleading his case, the interpreter was in trouble and the captain found her attractive. And why wouldn't he? She was stunning. Almost luminous. A pearl of great price. And she had been his, his, his. With eyes closed, he remembered their lovemaking in the glade. It was never going to last; he knew that. Perhaps it was just as well he had been captured. He never wanted to hurt Henni and his love for his wife hadn't faded or disappeared. This was like being offered chocolate in the middle of a diet: the irresistible taste of forbidden fruit.

Wanda had dismissed his idea that he was falling in love with her, but it was possible, wasn't it, to love two women at the same time? He hadn't pursued the matter, though. Why was that? Did he only want to be in love with her because it gave him permission to have sex? Was an adulterer a better man if love had prompted his actions rather than his body seeking pleasure? Either way, it didn't matter now. The longer their affair continued, the greater the chance of discovery; that would have made life at the farm impossible for both of them.

He imagined Henni's distress, her sense of betrayal; Gunter's disappointment in him for causing that distress;

the children's bewilderment, eventual understanding, and then rejection for hurting their Mama. It wouldn't matter if it happened years from now; he couldn't face his children's censure and he was certain it would be censure. No, it was better this way, even if it meant incarceration in one of those camps Alp had mentioned. It would be his punishment for transgressing his marriage vows; a punishment he would take if only he could keep his memories.

Wanda and the captain were deep in conversation; Wanda frowned and nodded and seemed to weigh something up in her mind. Lottie had moved alongside Gunter on the bench, her head on his shoulder. Henni was wringing her hands, glancing at everyone in turn. He smiled at her, trying to convey both courage and sympathy. It didn't seem to work.

'Right then, that's settled. If you could relay that information to the family, then we'll be away.'

Wanda turned to them and explained that she had been offered a post as an interpreter for the Army and had decided to take it.

'They'll be able to sort out identification papers for me, and I'll be paid as well. I think it's the right time for me to move on, but don't worry I'll stay in touch with you.'

'And Heinz?'

'They are going to take him in for further questioning.'

Tears ran down Henni's face.

'Don't worry, my dearest friend. I've already explained some of the background and how he helped people to the best of his ability. I've offered to make a statement vouching for him and I will not abandon him or any of you.'

Henni wiped her eyes and tried to pull herself together.

'Please say your goodbyes, while I put a few things together to take with me. That is, if it's all right for me to take the things you lent me?'

Minutes later, the jeep headed off. With the captain driving and Wanda in the seat next to him, the others were cramped in the back until they dropped the interpreter off at his village with the order to await further instructions. He glared at the jeep as it dove away.

'What's the next stage?' Wanda looked at the captain; she breathed more easily now the interpreter was no longer giving her the evil eye and muttering curses.

'We'll get back to base and place Bauer in one of our holding cells. Then we'll sort out accommodation and a pass for you. One of our intelligence people will handle the interrogation. They're all bilingual, so there'll be no need for an interpreter. And then, I hope you'll join me for dinner tonight?'

'Thank you. I'd love to.'

After a while, she asked if she could tell Heinz what was going to happen next.

'Be my guest.'

'Listen, Heinz, I'll be quick. I've said nothing about the railroaders. It's up to you whether you mention the den. I'll tell them my full story, and you can too, if you need to. Do not mention the glade. Looks like you'll be held at the army base and interrogated there.'

'You never told me you could speak English.'

'You never asked.'

And with that, she turned around and smiled at the captain.

'He OK in the back there?'

'Yes, he just wanted to know why I hadn't told him I spoke English.'

'Why didn't you?'

'He never asked.'

The captain burst out laughing and everyone, bar Heinz, entered the army camp in high spirits.

CHAPTER 21

IT WAS A BROWN room containing a wooden table and chairs. High metal windows cast light against the far wall. The cracked linoleum floor gave off a mouldy smell. He had spent a sleepless night pondering his fate. Should he tell them about the railroaders? Betray Alp and suffer the consequences? He couldn't make up his mind. Had he always been this indecisive? No. It wasn't possible to do his job as a detective and dither in this manner. What was wrong with him? He cast his mind back and saw himself riding a rollercoaster of emotions that had nothing to do with the image he had of a solid, unflappable family man.

There were footsteps in the corridor, and he sat up, chin raised. Wanda had promised to vouch for him and had already explained some of his background. How he longed to see her again. He couldn't very well ask for the privilege; maybe she would do so.

The door opened with the squeak of unoiled hinges. It spoiled the entrance of his interrogator, who filled the doorway, bloodshot eyes seeking his victim. The lengthy pause wasn't lost on Bauer; he'd acted in a similar fashion to unnerve his prey. He entered the room in two long strides and sat down; his colleague followed, closing the door before turning round to stare with open curiosity.

'I am Major Decker; this is Captain Johnson.' He spoke fluent German with a Saxon accent. His nicotine-stained fingers tapped the table. Bauer wondered if he was desperate for a cigarette or just impatient to be done with the entire process. The interrogation began with his Gestapo activities in Berlin.

'You are Inspector Heinz Bauer of the Gestapo. Yes, or no?'

'Yes.'

'You were based at the police headquarters at Alexanderplatz. Yes, or no?'

'Yes.'

'Not Prinz-Albrecht-Strasse 8?'

'No.'

'You joined the Gestapo in 1933, the same year you joined the Nazi Party. Yes, or no?'

'Yes.'

'The Gestapo or Secret State Police were integral to the Nazi regime. Yes, or no?'

'I suppose so.'

'Just answer yes or no.'

'Yes.'

'It had free rein to arrest and imprison suspects without recourse to the law. Yes, or no?'

'Yes.'

'Torture was used by the Gestapo to obtain confessions. Yes, or no?'

'Yes, but...'

'Just answer yes or no.'

'Yes.'

'Did you torture your prisoners?'

'No.'

'But some of your colleagues did?'

'Yes.'

'Nazi theory declared certain groups to be racially inferior. Yes, or no?'

'Yes.'

'These included Jews, Slavs, and Gypsies.'

'Yes.'

'These, among others, were the target of Gestapo investigations. Yes, or no?'

'Yes.'

'Many of the people arrested, interrogated and tortured by the Gestapo were then sent to concentration camps.'

'Yes.'

'Did you visit any concentration camps?'

'No.'

'Perhaps you should have done. Examine these photographs taken when we liberated Dachau concentration camp.'

Heinz leaned forward to bring them into focus, a stance of professional interest. After all, he was hardened to crime scene photography: newly found victims and dug up remains of ancient violations and murder. Wanda had described malnutrition, ill-treatment, death. He didn't expect rosy scenes, but nothing she had said prepared him for the searing images in front of him: skin stretched over living skeletons; huddled misery; mounds several feet high of decomposing corpses, eyes and mouths open in wordless anguish.

He slumped back; a thousand marching ants stung his body into an agony of hot and cold shivering; tears pricked his eyes and overflowed. His breathing became laboured. His heart weighed heavy. A sense of panic enveloped him.

'I didn't know…'

'You didn't know?' Voice curt, sarcastic; eyes narrowed.

'Please. I didn't know it was this bad.'

'How bad, exactly, did you think it was?'

'I don't know. Nothing like this.'

'And if you had known it was "this bad" would it have made any difference?'

He was an insect stuck to a display board; without the benefit of chloroform, he wriggled in pain and distress. What could he say? He wondered if anything he said would make any difference. They had already decided on their verdict. He was guilty; they all were. He remembered his conversation with Henni and understood what she meant.

'It was the smell that alerted them first. They thought they were downwind from a chemical factory. Acrid fumes like burning feathers off a plucked chicken or the bristles off a slaughtered pig. You ever done that? Now that you've exchanged Gestapo torture for farming freedom?'

'I never tortured anyone.'

'I didn't know… I never tortured anyone.' Decker parroted his words in a sneering tone.

'Before they reached the concentration camp, they came across a death train. Thousands left to die, left to rot. Corpses heaped on corpses. Sights and smells so disgusting that trained soldiers used to the horrors of the battlefield broke down in tears, vomited their guts out, went into shock.'

Motionless, Heinz stared at the floor. Time stopped. The room was silent; the only sound was the pounding of his heart.

'You have friends in high places. Yes, or no?'

'No.'

'Albrecht Hoffman is your brother-in-law, is he not?'

'Yes, but he's no friend of mine.' Frustrated by the endless yes or no, he squawked the words.

'Oh? What about your transfer to Krakow? Wasn't Hoffman instrumental in that move?'

'Yes.'

Despair shrouded him. If only they would let him explain; everything was being slanted the way they wanted to see things. He wasn't the man they were making him out to be. Is this how he had carried out interrogations? Ignoring the individual in front of him and fitting the evidence to suit the outcome he wanted?

'No!'

'You want to change your answer?'

'No. I'm sorry. I was answering a question in my head.' He hesitated, wondering if they would allow him to continue. 'I was wondering if I interrogated prisoners without letting them speak for themselves and my answer was no.'

The two men looked at each other, eyebrows raised.

'I wouldn't complain about your interrogation if I were you. Ask them if they could speak for themselves.' He pushed the photos across, his tone corrosive.

There was a young girl in the middle of the nearest photograph who looked just like Monika. They might have been twins. Unshorn, her hair lay about her face in gentle curls; her eyes and mouth closed in peaceful sleep. She couldn't have been at the camp long before they killed her. On top of her like an unholy blanket was an emaciated corpse, head stretched back, mouth and eyes wide open. Other pitiful corpses formed her mattress. What had she seen before she died? What had she suffered before they snuffed her life out?

Heinz sat with head bowed. He answered the rest of their questions without looking up. With the interrogation over, they led him back to his cell. He lay down on the canvas army bed and turned to the wall.

His mind raced as his body lay inert. This was worse than anything he had imagined. Faced with photographic evidence of Nazi crimes, he lost all sense of himself. Who was he? Who had he ever been? He tried on his different lives like a child dressing a doll: soldier; career detective; husband; family man; Gestapo officer; deserter; apprentice farmer; illicit lover. Was there anything linking these different people? Could he claim to be the same Heinz Bauer throughout? He felt stripped of everything he knew; naked, exposed. Even when he came back to the farm and saw his life in ruins, he still retained some sense of himself that made him want to fight on, to restore his relationship with Henni, to claim a future together. How did he come back from this? How did anyone come back from this?

He'd always hated the regime he worked for, subverted it by doing good whenever the opportunity arose. Now he understood how hollow that sounded to Allied ears. His job had made him part of an evil empire; what good was tinkering around the edges? He should never have joined the Party, never moved across to the Gestapo. He should have resigned and taken Henni back to her parents' farm. They would have survived. And his conscience would have been clear.

He heard Isaac's voice in his ear. "Don't cry out. I'll pull you back to safety." And he did, inch by tortuous inch, ignoring the gunfire, ignoring the snipers. And what did he do for Isaac? Nothing. How many times had he felt guilty? But what good was guilt if it didn't prompt you into action? A wasted emotion. The faces of his wife and children swam into view. He loved them and would do anything for them. More than that, he would do nothing to endanger them. Did they stand apart from the rest of humanity? Did protecting them mean ignoring the fate of other wives and children? If he had never married, never had children, what then? Would he have gone to stand alongside Isaac and his sisters?

As darkness descended, he started to hallucinate. His head grew larger; his body shrank. He resembled the corpses in the photographs. Images trapped in his mind whirled in a fast and furious dance, rending clothes and limbs, scattering blood and flesh. He was suffocating; mouth burning with acrid fumes. He was plummeting down into the abyss. Shadows moved in the surrounding night. He was empty. He had nothing to give them. A howl of anguish pierced his heart. The noise rose like waves crashing down on him. They were bellowing now, insistent, demanding, deafening.

'Cut it out in there.' There was a banging on the door. His mouth closed; the screaming stopped.

CHAPTER 22

'I THOUGHT YOU WERE a bit harsh on him, Sir, bearing in mind what we know about him.'

Major Decker stubbed out his cigarette and poured two more glasses from the nearly empty bottle of whisky.

'As far as I'm concerned, they can all rot in hell. You know my mantra: scratch the surface and you'll find Hitler in every single one of them.'

Johnson frowned. It was not an original concept. Armed Forces Radio constantly reminded them that "every friendly German civilian is a disguised soldier of hate… in heart, body and spirit every German is Hitler." He wasn't convinced: most of the civilians he came across seemed grateful to be rid of Hitler. Whatever enthusiasm they showed at the start of his dictatorship hadn't survived the years of war and ultimate defeat. He tried again.

'He moved across to the Gestapo as an Inspector and never advanced in rank. That says something, surely?'

'What exactly?'

'Well, if he were a committed Nazi, an enthusiastic supporter of their policies, you'd expect him to get promoted.'

'Maybe he was crap at his job.'

'That's possible, of course. I'm just saying he wasn't a major player, an instigator of anything.'

'Just doing his job, was he? Just a pen pusher? Come off it, Johnson. All this "I didn't know" doesn't wash with me. He was Gestapo, for goodness' sake. He was there when they were clearing the Jews out of Berlin. Don't tell me he witnessed that and believed they were all going off for a merry little picnic somewhere.'

'No, but by then he had little choice in the matter. Go along with the policy or find yourself in a concentration camp. He struck me as being full of remorse; ashamed of the rather small part he played in all this. His reaction to the photographs was genuine.'

'It's easy to be full of remorse when you're trapped in a corner with nowhere to go. Besides, nobody could be part of the Gestapo and claim to have played a "small part" in the war. You know as well as I do' – he paused to light another cigarette – 'the Gestapo were integral to the regime. Can't say I like any German, but the Gestapo and the SS were the real nasties. It's also insulting to those who had the guts to fight the regime, including women and children, many of whom ended up tortured by the Gestapo or left to starve in places like Dachau. No, Johnson, your sympathy is misplaced.'

He decided against pursuing the matter. The discovery of the concentration camps had changed everything: they were all convinced now they had been fighting Evil with a capital E rather than enemy troops. All the same, he had his doubts about the necessity for denazification of the entire population. War-weary and leaderless, what were they going to do? No doubt there were diehards unwilling to accept their dream of world domination was over, but most of the captured SS men and other Nazi officials they held in POW camps appeared broken rather than belligerent. He just didn't reckon it was practical to keep thousands upon thousands of men locked up while the bureaucratic cogs and wheels turned with their usual infuriating slowness.

Besides, there was a certain hypocrisy in condemning men like Bauer while rounding up Nazi industrialists, scientists and engineers to work for them in the States. Better working for them than the Russians, but the aftermath of war was proving just as murky as war itself.

Decker hadn't mentioned the killing of German guards, including those trying to surrender, by the traumatized troops who liberated the camp. A rare loss of discipline, it was true, but shaming. The large-scale bombing of Hamburg and Dresden may have been necessary to bring the war to an end, but it didn't contribute to the Allies' moral high ground.

How depressing it all was. Or was it working with Decker? The man never lightened up, never revealed the slightest shred of humanity; he was fuelled by whisky and cigarettes and never bothered with the officers' mess, either. Well, that was his business. He just hoped it didn't end up dragging him down.

It was time to meet up with his oldest buddy and his delightful new girlfriend; he wasn't looking forward to it. Decker wasn't likely to recommend Bauer for early release and he didn't see there was much he could do about it.

* * *

'But I don't understand. Bauer didn't join the Party until 1933, so he's not hard-core Nazi. He deserted his post to return home to his family, which could have seen him killed as a deserter. There hasn't been a single accusation of torture against him. Wanda's prepared to vouch for him, which must count for something seeing as she's one of the survivors of Auschwitz. It doesn't make sense.'

'I know. It's just a pity he's landed in Decker's in-tray. He's on a personal mission to eliminate each and every Nazi. And he's one of those men who hardens his stance the more you argue against him. I can't see what else I can do.'

'I must say, Wanda, you're taking it all calmly.'

'Something will turn up; something always does. It's the rest of the family I'm sorry for. Gunter must be getting on for 80. It's a time of life when you want to take things easy, no matter how robust you are. There's no pension for farmers so he's got to carry on as best he can. Plus, his wife has dementia and needs constant looking after. And you saw for yourself how exhausted Henni looks. The children are lovely, but there's only so much they can do to help around the farm. It makes me feel guilty that I left to take up this job. Perhaps I should resign and go back there?'

'Don't you dare! I'll have you arrested as a deserter.' He reached for her hand, smiling with wonder at her beauty and intelligence. 'We'll figure something out before too long. Like you said, something will turn up.

'Besides, you can't let the Colonel down. He's coming next week, and he needs a top-notch interpreter. We can't give him one of those chancers we've been forced to hire. I'm still of the opinion we should have charged that last interpreter with looting; still, at least he's got his comeuppance. He won't be working for us again.'

'Times are tough. He's probably got a family to feed and hunger drives people to do many things they would normally regret.'

'You're an amazing woman, Wanda. I reckon you've got the biggest heart of anybody I've ever met. After everything you've been through, you can still find it in you to understand other people and forgive them.'

'Perhaps everything I've been through makes that process easier?' She turned to Johnson. 'Do you suppose the Major would allow me to visit Heinz?'

'Probably not, but do you know what? I've had about as much as I can take of Decker for one day and, as he's not said anything to the contrary, I'll take you to see the prisoner myself.'

'You guys go ahead. I'll wait here for you, Wanda.'

* * *

Bauer lay motionless, facing the wall, as they entered the cell. The single light bulb barely illuminated the room. A mess tin and mug of water lay untouched on the floor.

'Get up, Bauer, you have a visitor.' There was a note of irritation in Johnson's voice as he considered the likely rebuke he would get for his actions and the man wasn't even responding, let alone showing any gratitude.

Wanda gestured for permission to approach Bauer and knelt alongside the camp bed.

'Heinz, it's me, Wanda.'

There was a grunt and Heinz emerged from the shadows; he moved like a man stuck in quicksand, fighting a force greater than his own. He shifted his legs over the side of the bed, levered himself up, and faced them.

His eyes were damp and empty; his unshaven face and tousled hair gave him the look of a tramp; there was a penetrating smell of sweat and despair.

'I'm so sorry, Wanda. I've seen what it was like now. There's no excuse for any of us. Henni was right. We don't deserve forgiveness. We don't deserve to live. I am so very sorry.'

He turned to lie down again. Wanda grabbed his arm and shook it.

'Look at me, Heinz. In all the time I've known you I've never taken you for a coward.'

'Oh, Wanda, but that's exactly what I was. I was a coward. I didn't stand up to Hitler or his henchmen. I made excuses for myself, for my actions. What good was helping people here and there when we were all drowning in the greatest evil we've ever known?'

'Were your children cowards too?'

'My children? No, of course not. You can't blame them. They're innocent. Please...' he turned a stricken face towards Johnson. 'They're innocent.'

'It's OK, Bauer. Stay calm. We accept your children are innocent.'

'If they're innocent, don't make them do penance for your crimes.' said Wanda.

'What do you mean?'

'They need their father now more than ever. A father to love them, to guide them in the long and painful years to come as we rebuild Germany into a better nation, one we can all be proud of.'

'Henni can do that. She's always done it and she's always been better at it than I am.'

'That's rubbish. Did you even say goodbye to your children before you left?'

'No, I didn't, but that's not my fault. They were away, staying with Hans and Clara.'

'Think how bewildered they are now. Their beloved Papa taken away. Think of your relationship with Monika, with Carola, with Tomas. If you sink into the pit of despair, you'll be making them pay the price. You're right to talk about us drowning in evil. Have you ever tried to rescue a drowning man? It's a dangerous business because you're just as likely to drown yourself as rescue him.

'You threw out lifelines to many people. You saved many people, and you did so without endangering your wife or children. That is a remarkable achievement and one you can be proud of.'

'It's kind of you to say so, Wanda, but I've been a shallow man all my life. I see that now. I was distracted by shiny baubles and easy pleasures and all too quick to pat myself on the back for the small things I achieved without ever considering the bigger picture. There are so many actions I regret now and will continue to regret for the rest of my life.

'I hid behind Henni and the children. I told myself I couldn't endanger them but that was my cocoon, my oh-so-convenient cocoon. When I think of the Great War, I see how I didn't engage with that either. It was always do what you need to do to survive. Forget acts of bravery. Forget acts of compassion. Just survive. But there has to be more to us than just survival. You have to break the cocoon, however painful that is, or you never grow, you never become what you are capable of.'

'It takes courage to face the past, Heinz, and I'm proud of you for doing that, but it takes even more courage to face the future. Think about the mountain Henni must climb. She's already exhausted and yet she now has to cope with Lottie, with bringing up the children, with organising the vegetable garden, with cooking and cleaning. Then there's Gunter, longing for retirement, yet unable to stop milking the cows, making the cheese, harvesting the hay. Think of your beloved children. They need you there, alongside them, a proper father figure who takes responsibility for his actions and steps forward day after day no matter what the personal cost. You can return to them a better and stronger man. I know you can and deep down you know it too.'

'Perhaps you're right. Perhaps I can still break the cocoon.'

He licked his bottom lip and held Wanda's gaze.

'I am right.' She reached for his hand and held it. 'I have been there. I have seen it for myself, and I am telling you, Heinz, that nothing is more important right now than you returning to your family and doing your duty alongside them. And you can start right now by eating your meal, inedible though it looks. Eat, sleep, exercise, and wait with hope and resolution for the day of your release.'

After several minutes, she shook his arm again. 'Promise me you'll do that. Promise.'

He sighed. 'Yes, all right, I'll try to do my best.'

'Thank you.' She leaned forward and kissed him on the cheek, then hugged him with all her might.

As they walked away from the cell, Johnson congratulated her. 'You did well in there. When I first saw his face, his whole demeanour, I thought we were going to have to put him on suicide watch.'

'I don't feel I did well at all. The way he looked and spoke shocked me, too. It was wrong to start talking about cowardice. I should have made him connect with his children straightaway. Let's hope he doesn't stay locked up for too long. The sooner he returns to his family, the sooner he'll recover.'

Johnson nodded in agreement; he didn't have the heart to tell her there wasn't a hope in hell of an early release.

CHAPTER 23

'I CAN'T SPARE THE time to go with you, but Jonesy here will drive you up to the farm, run some errands for me, and come back for you later. I'll see you tonight when you get back.'

With that, he peckeds her on the cheek and set about his duties. Wanda watched him go, turned to give Heinz a tender look, and climbed into the jeep. As they trundled through the countryside, she allowed herself a smile of pride and achievement. None of her colleagues had expected Heinz to be released so soon, but she always knew a colonel trumped a major. She'd proved her worth as an interpreter and then argued her case. It helped that the colonel had an eye for the ladies, and she'd been charm personified, knowing when to concentrate on the work in hand and when to flirt. It had been a fun time, and now she was looking forward to seeing the family again.

'Papa!' Screams of delight greeted Heinz as he descended from the jeep. The children ran forward and hugged him, all of them talking at once, telling him everything that had happened while he was away. He crouched down, hugging them, touching their faces, stroking their hair.

Henni stood in the doorway, eyes soft and damp, watching the reunion with deep contentment. Wanda came up to her and they hugged, needing no words. The children wouldn't let go of their father and wouldn't stop chattering away, interrupting each other and giving each other playful shoves to gain a better position and monopolise his attention.

When the excitement died down, they sat around the kitchen table and Heinz showed them his letter, signed by Colonel Hall, giving him permission to return to the farm, continue his work as a farm labourer and giving him immunity from further denazification procedures. There were several conditions attached: he wasn't to leave the area for any reason; he wasn't to apply for any other job; he wasn't allowed to use firearms of any description or for any purpose.

'It's a small price to pay,' said Gunter.

'Yes, indeed it is. Oh, Heinz, it's so good to have you home.' Henni reached for his hand and looked deep into his eyes. 'We can start afresh, move beyond the circumstances that conditioned us, that diminished us.'

'Prototypes for a new Germany?'

'Why not?'

Lottie sat at the table, scowling at him. From time to time, he turned to smile at her, but the scowl never went away. Everyone had greeted him with warm embraces; when he approached Lottie, she had shrunk back and bared her teeth.

'Who is he?' Her quavering voice silenced the room.

'It's all right, Mama, it's Heinz. You remember, it's my husband, Heinz.'

'No, it isn't.'

Sotto voce, Henni told him not to argue, as it only made matters worse.

'She'll either remember you in due course or she won't.'

'I don't like him. I don't want him here. Make him go away.'

The children looked at each other and started giggling.

'He can't go, Mama, he's staying for lunch.'

'No.'

'Listen, Henni, I've been cooped up for so long that I'd like to go for a long walk. Is that all right with you?'

'Can we come?' said the children.

'Not this time, children. I need you to help me prepare lunch for your father and remember we still have that special thing to do.'

The children jiggled in their seats with excitement. Heinz stood on the doorstep for several minutes, taking deep breaths of air so pure it made his lungs tingle; he visited the wood store and then he set off for the forest.

When he'd first come to the farm, he'd seen it in great blocks of colour: blue skies, green fields, brown cows, dark green forests. Now he saw everything afresh in all its tiny detail: blades of sharp grass, emerald shards whispering in the breeze; an azure sky above him; vanilla and dove grey clouds in the distance, interspersed with sapphire; pines, spruces, and firs, each dripping their own shade of green from olive to moss to artichoke and lime. Such beauty in a world that had known such pain.

He approached the den with determination. Inside,

the empty metal box lay open; the water bottle, drained, leant against the earthen wall. He wondered if Alp knew about his arrest or had worked it out. Either way, their contact was broken now and would remain so. He swung the axe and set about demolishing the den. The cracks of wood splintering energised him; he tore down the roof and threw aside the branches until there was nothing left of the hideout.

'And so, it ends.'

Heinz spun round. Alp stood in front of him, dressed in his SS uniform, pointing a Walther P38 at his chest. He felt calm as he faced death. The sense of failing as a man, as a human being, had overwhelmed him during his long hours in the prison cell. He would have welcomed any punishment meted out by the Allies, even death. Thoughts of his family flashed up, and a vague sense of regret made him swallow hard. It was his duty towards them that had forced him to make an effort; with Wanda's encouragement, he had resolved to make amends for his cowardice by living a good life henceforth. Now he felt irritated that a whining mosquito would deliver the final blow.

'Risky, don't you think, wearing an SS uniform nowadays?'

'But appropriate for an execution.'

'Haven't there been enough deaths?'

'Not of vermin. You never stop killing vermin. You should know that, living on a farm.'

'Human beings aren't vermin. Underneath our uniforms, our clothes, our hairstyles and fashions, we are all the same flesh and blood. We have the same needs.

We face the same problems. We desire the same things. The gun in your hand changes the dynamic between us, but it doesn't change the human nature we both share.'

Heinz was warming to his theme when there was a deafening crack, thump, crack, thump, followed by a final thud as Alp fell to the ground.

'Oh my God,' he said in a whisper as Gunter strode towards him, carrying his hunting rifle.

'Is he dead?'

'Yes.'

'Good, then help me bury him. I've prepared a pit at the edge of the meadow field. It should be deep enough to prevent scavengers from getting at him.'

Each grabbed an arm and dragged him down to the edge of the forest, where they followed the path to the field. Panting with exertion, they manoeuvred the body into the pit. Heinz paused to catch his breath, then picked up the spade lodged into the mound of soil and started filling in the grave.

'How did you know?'

'Tomas never stopped referring to him as "the bad man". When they arrested you, he asked if it was because of the bad man. That started me thinking. I trust your lad's instincts, so I kept a watch on the den. As chance would have it, I saw your man here give the Heil Hitler salute to somebody emerging from the den in the early hours of the morning, not long after you'd gone. I didn't know he was SS, but he was still fighting on behalf of that dead maniac.

'Do you remember that talk we had about cornered animals? Cornered or not, I knew he was dangerous. As long as he left my family alone, then I would leave him alone, but I would always be prepared for him.

'I didn't know if we'd ever see you again, but if I've learnt anything over the years, it's being prepared for all eventualities. A pit's always useful for dead stock, so I dug this ready. When you wanted to go for a walk, I guessed you would go to the den, so I followed you.'

'Thank God you did. He was planning to execute me. That's why he was wearing his uniform. To make it official in his eyes.'

'The bastard.' Gunter stared at the ground, running a hand through his hair. 'And I'm no better. I've just executed him, without a trial, without a chance to state his case or even make peace with his Maker.'

'If you hadn't, I'd be dead and who knows if he wouldn't have come after the rest of you, Tomas included.'

'Yes, put like that, it's hard to have any regrets. This stays between us, mind, now and forever.'

'Now and forever. What shall we do with the gun?'

'I'll go back for it later. Remember you're not allowed to handle firearms.'

Heinz laughed. 'I don't suppose I'm allowed to bury the enemy either.'

They walked back to the farm engaged in conversation like two old friends catching up on all the news and gossip.

Henni stood in the open doorway, twisting her wedding ring round and round.

'We heard the shots. What happened?'

'Your poor old father is losing his touch. We were

this close to having some venison for the larder, but all I did was shoot some trees.'

'So why are you so dishevelled and what's that soil on your trousers?'

'Heinz helped me give chase in case I'd injured him. He's not as fit as he was, stumbling all over the place just like a wounded stag himself.'

'All right, all right. There's no need to make so much of it.'

Henni smiled indulgently. 'Come inside and see what the children have prepared for you.'

The kitchen was decorated for a feast: the table laden with food; vases filled with flowers and greenery; streamers made from rags hung from the rafters; paper chains, cut out from old magazines, festooned the fireplace; three excited children stood dressed in their Sunday best, each holding a gift for their father.

'Welcome home, Papa.'

'We've got presents for you, Papa.'

'Open mine first.'

Heinz held out his arms wide and gathered them into a hug. 'My wonderful children. What would I do without you all?' Then he proceeded to ooh and ahh over his gifts: a poem written by Monica and decorated with flowers and birds; a drawing by Carola of a man holding a little girl by the hand with a bright sun shining in the sky; a twig whistle made by Tomas.

'Opa helped me with the whistle, but I did most of it myself. Look, this is how it works.' Tomas blew hard, and they all covered their ears.

'That's brilliant and very useful. Well done, Tomas.

Now do we have any frames so that I can put this wonderful picture and this very special poem behind glass to protect them?'

'I'm sure we can find something,' said Henni. 'Here, let me put them out of harm's way on the mantelpiece and then let's sit down to eat.'

With his family, including Wanda, seated around the table, he felt a deep sense of love spread through his body and radiate outwards. He ate, he chatted, he smiled and all the while waves of love bathed him in a celestial ablution. Born anew, he would grasp this second chance with all his might and humility. He would make each moment count; love would dictate his every move; and when his time came, he would die a contented man.

ACKNOWLEDGEMENTS

My grateful thanks to all the readers of my first draft for their kind words, wise comments and corrections: Barbara Dresner, Janet Hurton, Mick Jeffs, Jackie Lang, Geraldine Parker, Marta Pittarello, Jean Walters.

Particular thanks go to Jamie Pumfrey and Natasha Wielogorska whose insights greatly improved the book.

My friend Birgit Fischer provided me with the fictional village of Gerstenried and my husband Mike provided endless encouragement, support, and designs for the front cover.